## *Nobody else made her feel this way!*

Rafe Drayford had no right to come marching back into Caroline's well-ordered life. He had opted out and he should darn well have stayed out. Caroline was seething with righteous anger, bringing back the memory of the slap she'd given him. She had been confused then. Now her mind was clear, reason and instinct telling her that Rafe was out to wreck her peaceful existence and play havoc with the man she loved.

**Jane Donnelly** began earning her living as a teenage reporter. When she married the editor of the newspaper, she free-lanced for women's magazines for a while, and wrote her first Harlequin Romance as a hard-up single parent. Now she lives in a roses-around-the-door cottage near Stratford-upon-Avon, in England, with her daughter, four dogs and assorted rescued animals. Besides writing she enjoys traveling, swimming, walking and the company of friends.

# Sleeping
# Beauty
## Jane Donnelly

*Harlequin Books*

TORONTO • NEW YORK • LONDON
AMSTERDAM • PARIS • SYDNEY • HAMBURG
STOCKHOLM • ATHENS • TOKYO • MILAN
MADRID • WARSAW • BUDAPEST • AUCKLAND

ISBN 0-373-17278-8

SLEEPING BEAUTY

First North American Publication 1996.

**Printed in U.S.A.**

# CHAPTER ONE

WHEN she had planned this trip to Crete Rafe Drayford had certainly not entered Caroline's mind. He rarely did. Christopher's black-sheep elder brother had gone from the family circle long before Caroline had entered it.

She knew about him, of course. Everyone around here knew about Rafe Drayford, but Christopher hardly ever mentioned him. When he did he made it clear that so far as he was concerned the longer his brother stayed away the better. He would have preferred a complete break. It irritated him that his mother kept in touch with Rafe, and this suggestion that Caroline should seek him out and report back on him put Christopher into a state of frustrated fury.

She had not been anxious for the task herself but in the end, when Mrs Drayford had been pressing the letter on her, she had had to say, 'Well, if I'm that way I'll try to find him.' And here she was now, in the highland village that had been given as Rafe's last address, and although she was heading for the White Mountains herself she had put herself out to get here.

She could have said she couldn't find him or she hadn't come this way. That would have pleased Christopher, and as she had not left him on the best of terms perhaps she should be thinking of pleasing him. The trouble was that once the name came up and the letter was handed to her she had begun to wonder what Rafe Drayford was doing these days.

A brilliant law degree only qualified him for specialist work that he didn't seem to want, and Christopher had no idea how his brother was making a living. Nor, he said, had his mother.

The occasional letters that came for Mrs Drayford were brief. Any addresses were usually abroad, and although she always wrote back she had never risked her husband's wrath by flying out to find their son. But his latest letter had the name of a village and, as she told Caroline when neither of her menfolk was around, this could be a marvellous opportunity to find out what was happening from someone who would keep anything she did discover in the family.

Caroline had friends who would have been thrilled to hear the latest gen on Rafe Drayford, but Mrs Drayford was relying on her discretion. With Caroline of course there would be no gossip, no scandal.

Christopher's mother and father quite approved of Caroline, although the Hammonds were not on the Drayford's social level and Mrs Drayford was a raging snob. But that was the first time that Caroline had been treated to confidences about Rafe—or anything else— and certainly the first time that Christopher's mother had embraced her warmly when she said goodbye.

It had always been a cool kiss on the cheek before, but when Caroline had left to fly to Crete Mrs Drayford had hugged her, smiling into her eyes like a conspirator.

Now as she climbed out of her hired car, after a bone-shaking ride over a track strewn with boulders and potholes, Caroline wondered what Rafe Drayford was looking like. Nearly five years was long enough to have changed his appearance so that it might not be that easy to recognise him at first sight.

Four years ago he had been tall, dark and handsome in a moody fashion, overshadowing the fairer, slighter Christopher, who was two years younger and a head and shoulders shorter.

When Rafe was at home he had always caused a flutter among the local women, although he had a reputation for being unapproachable, sometimes downright arrogant, and everybody knew that he and his father didn't hit it off.

The Drayfords lived in Virginia Grove, a small manor-house. They were land- and property-owners and the law firm that Robert Drayford headed had an international reputation. Christopher was a solicitor with the firm now and Rafe had joined it briefly, but after a row with his father that had ended in Robert Drayford roaring, 'Get out of my house,' loud enough for everyone in the twenty-odd-roomed house to hear him, Rafe had walked out of the Grove and the village and never come back.

The last time Caroline had seen him had been at a garden fête on the lawns of the Grove in aid of the church restoration fund. The girl with him was from another wealthy family, with smooth hair and dressed like a top-rank model. She had had her hand through his arm, and her smug smile, as well as her clutching fingers, had said, Look what I've got!

Caroline, who had been helping on the tombola, had thought, No, you haven't; because she could see the restlessness in him. It gave him a dangerous glittering look so that she had half expected him to shake the girl's hand off his arm and stride off there and then, and it had been only a few days later that he had stridden out of the Grove.

Much later, when Christopher and Caroline had

become very good friends, Christopher had told her
that the girl had been heartbroken. Rafe had let her
down badly, without any warning, never bothering to
get in touch again. And he had told her, after she had
promised not to breathe a word of it, that missing
money had been the final straw that had made their
father order Rafe out of his home and out of their
lives.

Everything that Caroline had been told showed that
Rafe Drayford was a man who didn't give a damn for
anyone but himself. She hadn't liked him in the old
days for all his brooding good looks, and she didn't
expect to like him now. But she did have this letter to
deliver and she was curious.

It had been a lonely ride from the small hotel she
had booked into yesterday. That had been almost
empty, and so had the coastal town that swarmed with
tourists in the summer months. There was not much
traffic on the main roads and since she had taken the
track to this village, built on a ledge where the mountains started to rise, goats and sheep had been the only
sign of life. The village itself seemed eerily deserted.

She had reached a clearing where a huge plane tree
grew and a spring of water bubbled sluggishly and
between the houses alleyways seemed to lead into a
warren of lanes. But most of the houses were shuttered
and the doors of a white church, with its little bell
tower, were closed. Another car and a van under the
tree, looked near wrecks.

Outside her car the chill in the air struck her, making
her glad of her warm zipped-up coat. She wrapped a
long fleecy red scarf around her ears and dug her
gloved hands deep into her pockets, clutching her
shoulder bag under an arm. This could be a wasted

journey. He could be in any of these quiet houses, or in none; gypsying around seemed to be his way of life.

There were no details; not even the street name was given. All she could do was ask whoever she came across and all she had was his name—if he was using that and hadn't taken on a new identity. She should have asked his mother for a photograph—if his father hadn't insisted on a ceremonial bonfire of all his photographs years ago. Then she could have produced it and everyone would presume she was a deserted woman tracking a run-away husband or lover.

They would probably think that anyway, and it didn't matter to her whether she found him or not, although she would try to for his mother's sake. But she was on a voyage of discovery of her own, following the trail of a man who had died long before she was born, and this was like a trial run before she started on her real reason for flying to Crete.

If Rafe Drayford was still here somebody should know, and surely somebody would be appearing before long? If not she would start knocking on doors, using her smattering of Greek.

She went across to the church and tried the iron rope handle. When the door moved inwards she pulled up her scarf to make a head covering before she stepped inside. Nearer the altar the shadows were held at bay by the light from a few candles, and around the walls painted frescoes of haloed saints stared gloomily down.

She dropped in a coin and lit a candle. She remembered that St Anthony was supposed to be the saint for finding lost property, so perhaps she should be asking for help, but her candle was burning in an alcove containing the icon of a woman.

She could be the Madonna or the patron saint of the

village. She held a pitcher from which she appeared to
be pouring water, and Caroline knelt on the hard stone
floor and said a short silent prayer. She needed a
blessing. This was a crazy mission. Not the search for
Rafe Drayford—that was no more than a minor hitch.
But the whim that had suddenly become an obsession,
bringing her here at the worst possible time of year.

She turned round and stood up, hearing the soft-
footed approach of a man, bearded, in a long black
cassock and cone-shaped hat, with the same dark
haunted eyes as the frescoed saints. The priest might
know who was a newcomer in his village, and she
smiled and said, 'Rafe Drayford; I'm looking for him.'

'Ah!' He sounded as if he recognised the name. Then
he beckoned 'follow me,' and this could be incredible
luck.

She followed him across the clearing, where two
other men had materialised in the last five minutes,
and a few yards down one of the alleyways. There he
indicated the door of a terraced house, smiling as if he
thought she would be a pleasant surprise for the man
who was lodging there, and she tried out her Greek,
saying '*Efharistó*,' which she hoped was 'thank you'.

It seemed to be because he beamed at her, nodded
'you're welcome,' and was back in the square while she
still stood in front of the door with its peeling blue
paint.

She was relieved that it had been so easy; she didn't
want to waste her time chasing after Christopher's
brother, but the speed of her success had taken her
breath away. One minute she hadn't known where to
start looking, the next Rafe Drayford was probably
behind that door, and all she had to do was knock and
confront him.

'A letter from your mother,' she would say. 'She wants to know how you are.'

That would be it. Mission accomplished. She had hardly spoken to him before. She had been in her last year at school when he left, and although she had seen him riding through the village, driving through, and on the rare occasions when villagers were invited into the Grove, all she really knew about him was hearsay. But none of it was reassuring to somebody who was about to burst into his hideaway. If he had wanted anyone turning up, seeing for themselves what his circumstances were, he would have given an address, so he was not going to thank her for tracking him down.

The wind blew colder still and she pulled the scarf tighter over her head before she took off her glove and rapped on the door. The worst he could do was throw her out and she didn't want to stay anyway, so here goes, she thought; and when a man called something in Greek she presumed was 'come in', she lifted the latch.

The room was bigger than she had expected. Painted canvases were stacked against the white walls, and the effect was like that of the candles in the church, bright and burning.

She had remembered he was tall but he seemed taller still, and broader in the shoulders. His dark hair was longer, curling behind the ears and below the collar of his dark blue shirt. He wore breeches and jackboots and needed a shave.

When he saw her his eyes narrowed, and she pulled the muffling scarf off her head, shaking her dark red hair free, and said, 'It's Rafe, isn't it?'

Of course it was, and she thought, slightly hysterically, If his mother's worried about his health I can tell her he's in very good condition, if she doesn't mind him looking like a bandit.

'Yes,' he said. 'Who are you?'

'Caroline Hammond.'

He looked hard at her, then said, 'So it is.' She hadn't expected him to remember her. She had changed from a gawky schoolgirl to an elegant woman, from the daughter of a village shopkeeper to the daughter-in-law-to-be of the man who owned most of the village.

'So what are you doing here?' he asked.

'I came to give you this.' She took the letter out of her shoulder bag.

He thanked her, opened and read it, and from his expression of cynical amusement she was not sure that she wanted to be the one to take back a reply. 'Personal delivery,' he said, 'but you haven't flown here to hand this over. What *are* you doing here?'

'I'm on holiday.'

'Going where?'

'Into the mountains.'

'In this weather?'

It was cold. It was winter. But the mountains were where her path lay, although she had no intention of telling him that. She said, 'Perhaps not.'

'You're not on your own?' He grinned suddenly. 'Is my young brother waiting for you outside?'

No, Christopher was not, although he might have been. After the argument over whether or not she should go to Crete Christopher had announced that he would go with her. She hadn't objected. It needed not be a solitary pilgrimage, although Christopher couldn't understand how she had suddenly got the idea into her head or why it was so urgent.

Bookings had been made for both of them, and he had even said he would deliver Rafe's letter himself if he could find him, so that Caroline could stay out of it. But then, two days before they were due to leave, something had turned up—somebody falling ill and Christopher having to deputise so that the only option was cancellation.

Temporary, of course. For a month or two, maybe until the spring when the weather would be better. He could not have realised how passionately Caroline wanted to take this trip. She realised herself that she was not being reasonable, or she would never have started wondering if Christopher was determined to block any real contact with Rafe.

His colleague's perforated ulcer was genuine, but she did wonder if Christopher might have offered rather than been ordered to stand in for him, and if they had gone together whether he would have handed that letter to his brother or destroyed it.

She couldn't believe any of that, but she did know that she wasn't going to be disappointed and she set about arranging to fly out alone.

Christopher was not at home when she went up to the Grove the night before to say she was off in the morning, but Mrs Drayford saw no reason at all why Caroline should not take her little holiday. Christopher had never really wanted to go. He hated the cold and he did have this weak chest, and Caroline had the letter, hadn't she? And she would find the little village and look up Rafe?

Caroline had phoned Christopher's Birmingham hotel as soon as she booked into her own hotel in Crete, and left him a placating message. She hoped it would placate him because she loved him, and as soon as she had worked this restiveness out of her system she would be flying back to his arms.

If Rafe thought Christopher was with her now he must know how things were between them, and she asked, 'You know about Christopher and me?'

He held up the letter, one sheet of paper written on one side. 'My mother speaks highly of you; you seem to have passed the test.'

It had been a test. They had dated for several months before Christopher took her home and by then she knew that his parents had discussed her and decided that Caroline Hammond was acceptable. They would probably have preferred money with her but, after all, the Drayfords were loaded.

She murmured, 'That's kind of her.' When he smiled, his teeth were very white against a skin that had tanned to deep bronze since she had last seen him. He looked older, tougher, no longer the angry young man. She had thought he might be angry at her intrusion, but she seemed to be amusing him.

'It's not much of a compliment,' he said. 'The young women my parents approve of can be thick as two short planks so long as they make the right noises and look expensive.'

She nearly laughed, because it was true. The Drayfords did put appearances above everything, but she managed to stay cool, drawling, 'You think so?' and his eyes were still gleaming with laughter.

'You look exactly right. You'll fit into the Grove perfectly.'

It was a beautiful house, full of exquisite things, and Caroline, with her smooth shining hair, pale, clear skin and fine bone-structure, looked like a young lady of the manor. Which meant absolutely nothing.

'I'm a working girl,' she said.

'Are you, now? And what do you work at?'

'In a clothes shop.' It wouldn't mean anything to him if she told him that she was manageress for a very exclusive dress shop in the nearest town to her home village. 'And how are you earning a living?' She looked around at the canvases. 'Do you paint?'

'No,' he said with heavy irony, 'I'm minding them for a friend. Of course I paint.'

She was no art critic. These did seem to be amazingly good, but he had practically called her as thick as two short planks so she was not going to show she was impressed by his work. 'Are you any good?' she drawled.

'You wouldn't know? That's fine, you don't need any opinions of your own to be a Drayford.'

'Well, do they sell?' She added tartly, 'There are too many for them to be going like hot cakes.'

'Oh, they keep body and soul together.'

He was no starving artist. The hard, taut muscles rippled beneath his shirt, and she said, 'Your mother will be pleased about that. So will Christopher.'

'I'm sure he will,' he said drily, and she should not have mentioned Christopher because Rafe knew that Christopher wanted no news of him. 'So where is he?' he asked.

'In Birmingham today, on a libel action.'

'That should put the frighteners on them.' He didn't think Christopher was capable of frightening anybody, although how could he know when it was years since they'd met? 'So he's in Birmingham and you're here. Alone?'

'Yes, he wanted to come but he had to cancel.'

'Of course.'

'What does that mean?'

'I make him nervous. I'm surprised he let you near me.'

He must mean he used to make Christopher nervous, and she was sure he did. Nobody took much notice of Christopher when Rafe was around. Christopher still resented that bitterly, and Rafe was still contemptuous of his younger brother. She nearly blurted 'Well, you're not so bloody clever now compared with him, are you?' but the door opening saved her from that as a young woman carrying a large terracotta jug came into the house.

She was strikingly good-looking, tall and slim with a thick plait of dark hair hanging down her back, dressed in a black dress and wearing heavy gold earrings; and her start of surprise at seeing Caroline was obviously put on. She'd known Rafe had a caller.

Caroline wondered if she lived here. She had strolled in as if she did, and she must be one of the best-looking women around, the kind he would choose. He spoke to her, and all Caroline could understand was her own name, but the girl smiled and Rafe said, 'This is Elpida,' and Caroline said,

'Hello.'

'*Hérete*,' said Elpida, and carried her jug through the archway at the end of the room into what looked like a kitchen.

She came back with the jug empty and said something to Rafe, and he said, '*Ne*,' which meant yes. And surely meant, Come back later, because she went towards the door into the street and turned before she opened it, smiling a mischievous smile and fingering the beautiful earrings.

He gave her those, Caroline thought. Recently. This

may be the first time she's worn them. She said, amused, 'So I can tell your mother you're comfortable here?'

'Very comfortable. If you're here as my mother's spy.'

'I wouldn't put it like that.' She was, of course. When she got back Mrs Drayford would be waiting for every scrap of information, although none of it would reach anyone else. Robert and Christopher Drayford didn't want to know, and Caroline couldn't see Anna Drayford sharing this with her friends.

'And I'd thought you were bait,' he said.

'*What*?'

'Read the letter.'

He put it down on a table by the palettes and jars of brushes and tubes of oil paints. That, an easel and a stool were the only furniture this side of the archway. Now he picked it up again and offered it to her, and she really wanted to say, It's none of my business. But what *had* the woman written?

Rafe, I hope this letter finds you. I hope you are well. Little changes here, but I should be happy to see you again and so would your father if you returned prepared to meet him halfway. . .

What a chilly little note, Caroline thought. Sounds like something she might send to an ex-employee she was offering a second chance.

But it did warm up slightly. She missed him. She worried about him, and Virginia Grove was where he should be, with his family, among his friends. With a girl like Caroline, who would be marrying his brother in the spring.

Caroline was delivering this letter and she was a

lovely girl. 'If you came home, Rafe, you would find someone like Caroline. . .'

She put the letter down and said, 'Oh, dear.'

'Ridiculous,' he said. It was horribly embarrassing, although there was no need for him to go on, 'Considering I had an English rose and one of the reasons I cleared off was the prospect of spending the rest of my life with her.'

That was the girl at the garden party, and Caroline said tartly, 'Good for her, I should think. If I remember, she looked too good for you.'

'She looked like you.' She gasped. 'Very like you,' he said. 'When you walked in here, before you took the scarf off your head, I thought you were Isabel.'

The girl at the garden party had had fair hair. Caroline's was red, so dark that it could look black, a strong colour that made her skin seem even paler. With her hair hidden she might have had a slight resemblance to the girl Rafe had left behind, whose heart Christopher said he had broken. There would have been no welcome for Isabel here, and Caroline said, 'So that was the reason for the steely stare. Thank God that poor girl didn't turn up and it was only someone who didn't want to come and can't get away fast enough. You've got your letter. Good day to you. And don't hurry back—I don't know who these friends are your mother mentions because I've never met anyone who's missing you.'

He was between her and the door. She had to pass him to get to it and as she reached him he said, 'You're missing your chances with this assignment.'

'What chances? What assignment?'

'What can you tell her? The house, the paintings, a jug of soup from a neighbour. She'll expect more than

that. Won't she want to know about my mistresses, if
I've been in jail?'

'None of which would surprise me.' She was sure he
had mistresses. Like the kindly neighbour with the jug
of soup, flipping the earrings that celebrated something
steamily sexual. And he could have been in jail. Or
should have been. He looked like a villain. 'But no,'
she said, 'I don't think she would want to know that.'

He laughed, and although she was fuming, an image
of Mrs Drayford's expression if Caroline went back
and told her her son was an ex-con did have its funny
side. She wouldn't believe it. She certainly wouldn't
discuss it. She could well blame Caroline for stirring up
unpleasantness.

'She never wanted the grim facts about anything,' he
said. 'But I would like to hear what's been happening.'
That made her hesitate. 'Share my soup,' he suggested.

She had been nearly at the door, and perhaps she
should still walk out, but she could give him some news
of home if he wanted it and she was still curious about
him. 'Or do I make you nervous too?' he said.

He could have been overpowering. The dangerous
aura he had always projected was stronger than ever.
She thought he could make almost anyone nervous if
he chose, but she could hardly run away, and she said
coolly, 'No, you do not.'

'So you'll stay?'

'Why not?'

He went towards the kitchen and for the first time
she began to take note of her surroundings. She had
seen the paintings, the table, but all her attention had
been centred on the man. Now she looked around, at
the hard-beaten earthen floor, the ladder steps leading

to rooms under the roof, at the rough-hewn beams of
the ceiling.

Through the archway there was a stove set in what
had been an open hearth, a table and rush-bottomed
chairs, and hanging from the beams were strings of
onions, herbs, dried tomatoes.

In the summer this would be a green and leafy village
and the house would have a rugged charm. But now
the village seemed bleak and barren and in the house,
although the stove was burning and heat radiated from
the stones around it, she was chilly. She unzipped her
coat but kept it on, and was glad that the soup he had
poured from an iron pot into the bowls was hot.

It was a thick onion and chickpea soup, filling and
warming, and she said, 'This is good; compliments to
the chef.'

'I'll pass them on,' he said.

'Do you cook for yourself?' She was making conversation; she didn't know how much of this harsh lifestyle
Mrs Drayford would want to hear about.

'Occasionally,' he said.

More often than not she felt there would be a woman
in his kitchen, or bringing him his meals, keeping his
house clean, making his bed, sharing his bed.

There was bread, cheese, butter and a jug of wine
on the table. He filled her tumbler with a cloudy brown
liquid and she tasted it gingerly. She had tasted worse.
If she got this down she might end up cross-examining
him like the lawyer he used to be.

'You paint,' she said.

'I paint.'

'Did you always want to paint?' She hadn't heard
that, but those who might have known never talked

about Rafe in front of the family and Caroline was family now.

'There wasn't much time for it in the old days,' he said.

'What have you been doing all these years?'

'Travelling. What have you been doing?'

'Staying around,' she said. 'Never really going anywhere.'

He waited as if he had caught something wistful in her voice, but that was all she was saying, and after a few minutes he said, 'Four years, coming up to five since you were manning that tombola stall.'

'Yes.' She hadn't known he had noticed her, but it had been his last public appearance, so maybe details had stayed in his mind, and when she smiled he waited again and this time she did explain. 'I thought you looked like a cross between Lord Byron and Mr Darcy that day—I was taking English Literature A level at the time, so that was how my mind worked.'

'A pair of arrogant bastards,' he said.

'You said it.'

'And now?'

She laughed. 'Now you look more like Heathcliff on a rough day. If you turned up at the Grove like this Mrs Drayford would probably have a fit.'

'I should shave,' he said. 'I usually do. I wasn't expecting company.'

'You were expecting Elpida.'

'Elpida doesn't have your delicacy.' He rubbed the stubble on his jawline. 'This wouldn't scar her.'

'She has beautiful skin,' said Caroline. 'And *exquisite* earrings.' The way she stressed that told him that Elpida's gesture had been understood. 'You and Elpida are. . .?' She paused, raising smooth winged brows.

'Yes,' he said.

'Do I tell them that back home?'

'Tell them what you like,' he said. 'Now tell me. . .'
And from then on he was doing the questioning.

He asked about her parents, who were still running
their grocery store although her father had been trying
to sell and retire for the last six months. Then he went
round the stallholders at that garden fête and she told
him what had happened to them: who had died,
married, left the village, changed jobs, who still lived
in the same homes, doing the same jobs.

She was surprised he remembered them all. After
nearly five years she couldn't even recall if Christopher
had been at the fête, although she remembered Rafe
vividly. She told him what she knew about the names
he came up with and he listened attentively, but she
knew he was not going home. He was interested but
not homesick, and that was sad, because he and
Christopher were brothers and it was sad that the gulf
between them should be so wide and so unbridgeable.

Then he asked, 'And what happened to you, after
the tombola?'

'Not a lot.' She laughed at herself because on the
surface a great deal had happened to her. 'I went as a
salesgirl to the shop where I'm still working as manageress. It's a stylish shop. Your mother's always been a
very good customer.'

After Caroline's third date with Christopher
Drayford Mrs Drayford had come into the shop and
Caroline had served her. She had always been gracious,
if sometimes patronising, and that day the change in
her manner was so slight that only Caroline was aware
of it. She chose an expensive new outfit, with her usual

eye for what suited her, but she watched Caroline some of the time instead of her own reflection all of the time.

She had seen Caroline dozens of times over the years, never really looking at her, but today she was sizing her up, and Caroline—wearing a couture suit herself, bought on staff discount—thought that she might have gone home to the Grove and told her husband, 'The girl is fairly presentable.'

Now she told Mrs Drayford's other son, 'Everything's gone smoothly for me; I've been lucky.'

'And how did you and Christopher get together?'

Christopher would hate to think of her sitting here, sipping wine with Rafe and discussing their love-affair with him, but she supposed it was a natural enough question. 'We did a fashion show at the Grove and I did the commentary,' she said. 'It was for charity; your mother does a lot for charity.'

'Born committee woman, my mother,' he agreed. 'Never gets her hands dirty but she's very caring on a platform.' That certainly summed up Anna Drayford, although Caroline felt she ought to be protesting in some way, but he went on, 'You looked good as the compere, of course, and that was how it happened, was it? Christopher, seeing you in the right setting and knowing you were the right girl?'

The drawing-room and the conservatory had provided a perfect background for the models in their beautiful clothes, and Caroline had been a charming and competent hostess; and it was later that day that Christopher had asked her if she was interested in a show that he had tickets for.

From then on they had dated steadily, but yes, that was when he had probably decided he liked the look of her. She shrugged and said silkily, 'Could be. Did

Elpida see you here and say, "Bingo"—or whatever
that is in Cretan—"Here comes my mountain man"?'

When he began to laugh so did she. The wine was
potent as a liqueur and when she got back she could
tell his mother that Rafe might be roughing it but he
was doing what he wanted, getting what he wanted.
And always would if Caroline was any judge, because
he had the strength and confidence of a man who could
handle and control his own destiny.

'Talking of mountains,' he said, 'why are you going
up into the mountains alone?'

'Just a fancy.' But he persisted,

'Why? Have you been there before? Did you read a
book about it? What's the attraction?'

She hacked off a piece of bread from the loaf with a
bone-handled knife that would have made a handy
weapon, and spread it with butter while she was
deciding that she might as well explain because he was
not going to believe a motiveless whim.

'My grandfather was here during the war with the
Resistance,' she said. 'He was a wireless operator.'

'They were brave men.' He was silent for a moment,
then he asked, 'But why not come in the season when
you could take the tours, travel in comfort?'

'I don't want comfort. I just want to go where he
went without crowds being around.'

'I strongly advise you to go back home and wait for
the spring.'

'I'm getting married in the spring.'

He looked at her quizzically. 'What's that got to do
with it?'

'Nothing.' Or everything, because it was when a date
had been set for the wedding that the restlessness had
started.

After she was married Caroline Hammond would be Caroline Drayford, the daughter around Virginia Grove and no longer her own woman. It was a future most women would envy, but when she was alone she had looked at the faded photograph of her grandfather, who had died only a few years older than she was now, and her own life seemed safe and sheltered with no risk or danger in it.

She had never had to struggle for anything. Not even love. The most eligible man in the district had chosen her, and he was handsome and loving and she would have felt the same about him if he hadn't had a penny to his name. She wanted to marry him and be with him always. But she thought, I would like to see where my grandfather lived for four years.

Her roots were in a quiet English village, but there had been a time of passion and heroism in the high mountains of Crete that was part of her heritage too. She didn't know what she would be looking for but suddenly it had become imperative that she should make this journey.

When she had told Christopher she was taking some time off and going to Crete he had thought she meant to stay in a resort, and when she had said, 'I want to go into the White Mountains,' Anna Drayford had put down her magazine and said eagerly,

'But that's where Rafe is. . .'

'Just how were you proposing to set about this jaunt?' Rafe was asking her now.

'I thought I'd get a guide. I have the names of some of the villages. Well, I think I have. And the names of some of the men who were with him.'

'Fifty years ago.'

'I know that.' She tried to eat a piece of bread but it

crumbled in her throat, making her cough and take another gulp of wine before she could go on. 'I'm only going on what my grandmother told me, what he'd told her, and that was years afterwards when she was an old woman herself. She died a while ago. He came home once for a few weeks during the war, and then went back and didn't come home again.'

The look he was giving her was almost pitying. 'The hamlets on the peaks are deserted now. You couldn't make it.'

'Why not?'

She had slipped off her coat and slung it over the back of her chair. He reached for her hand and pushed up the sleeve of her sweater. Her fingers were long with white-tipped manicured nails, and her slender wrist looked as if his grip could snap it.

But she had always been much stronger than she looked, she had steel in her and she controlled the urge to jerk her arm away and said, 'I'll get where I want to get; I always do.'

That was a stupid challenging boast, and he looked down at the antique ruby cluster Christopher had given her when they had got engaged. 'I'm sure you do,' he drawled. 'But the mountains would call for a different kind of stamina.'

Angry colour burned in her cheeks—she had in no way schemed for an engagement ring—and he smiled into her flushed face with the full lips set stubbornly. 'But if you're determined——' he said.

'I am.'

'I'll take you.'

'As a guide?'

'I've lived here long enough to take you where you

want to go, as far as you can make it. We'll turn back when you've had enough.'

He thought that would be within hours, but she would have to be half dead before she would give up as soon as he expected. She was no mountaineer but she was agile and fit, and she could understand why Christopher resented him so fiercely—his arrogance was intolerable. Who the *hell* did he think he was?

'Why should you go to the trouble of acting as my guide?' she demanded.

He was still holding her hand, so lightly that she hardly felt the touch, but if she moved back she would have to pull away and it was easier to pretend he wasn't holding her.

'You're almost my sister-in-law,' he said softly. 'For Christopher's sake I should be looking after you.'

Her ring was ruby-red, blood-red, and she was remembering that blood feuds still raged in these wild regions. Rafe Drayford looked like a mountain man, and it was nearer hate than love betwen him and his brother. His hand seemed to close around her wrist, and suddenly she felt less like a casual caller delivering a letter than a hostage.

# CHAPTER TWO

As soon as Rafe loosed her hand Caroline resisted an impulse to rub her wrist as if he might have bruised it. That was nonsense, his grip could hardly have been lighter, but she took another good gulp of wine because she did need steadying down.

Getting a flare of panic because he was offering to be her guide into the mountains made no sense at all. It was a great idea. If he'd been here long enough to know his way around she was lucky there.

She hadn't told anyone that she would have been looking for a guide, going off with a strange man on a lonely trek. If she had her parents and the Drayfords would have thought she was mad and there would have been a stand-up row before she got away. If she got away. Well, now she had a family escort, which wouldn't please Christopher, although he might possibly prefer his brother to a stranger.

Better the devil you know, she thought, and realised that the wine was going to her head. There was certainly something devilish about Rafe Drayford; the eyebrows for a start. But he was a stranger to her; she hardly knew him at all.

'Tell me what your grandmother told you,' he said.

She hadn't even written it down. Her father's mother had been a frail and gentle woman who had lived with them until she died quite suddenly when Caroline was thirteen. She had been a war widow, but her husband had not come from their small town, and although

Caroline knew he had served with the partisans in Crete and been killed in the weeks before the island was liberated, it seemed to her now that it was on just the one evening that her grandmother had talked about his time in the White Mountains.

They had been alone in the little parlour behind the shop and Caroline had been reading a travel brochure and said, 'I'd like to go to Crete. Wouldn't you?'

Her grandmother had raised faded blue eyes from something she was stitching and said, 'No.'

That wasn't surprising. Her grandmother was a homebody; the annual family seaside holiday was enough for her. But Caroline had remembered, 'Isn't that where my grandfather was in the war? What was it like? What happened there?'

She was twelve years old, a bookish girl, and it was like a stumbling history lesson when her grandmother had begun to search her memory for what she had been told many years ago by a young man who would never grow old.

Caroline had listened, enthralled, and when her parents had come back from the cinema and her grandmother had gone back to her sewing she had asked, 'Will you tell me more about Crete some time?'

'That's all I know,' her grandmother had said.

Now Caroline was the one stumbling, and the place names she was trying out weren't getting much response. She explained again, 'It's just word of mouth, what she remembered that he'd said.'

Then she said one and Rafe said, 'That was destroyed, but it's been rebuilt after a fashion.'

'Cave of the Winds.' She was sure of that. You would remember that. But he shook his head again.

'You've had that one. It's inaccessible as far as you're concerned.'

She wouldn't argue. She couldn't shin up precipices but she would still get further than he expected. 'His name?' he asked.

'Sergeant Daniel Hammond. He was here during the Battle of Crete but he stayed behind during the evacuations. He was a wireless operator and he worked with the Resistance. I've got pictures of him in my case in the car.'

He pushed back his chair. 'I'll get them.'

She dug her keys out of her bag and handed them over. 'It's the hire car under the cypress tree, a jeep.' Although he was hardly likely to mistake it for the couple of wrecks that must have been there for months.

He would be bringing back her case, and if they were leaving from here she would have to be staying here tonight at least. Not in this house, she thought. She would have to look for lodgings. The village had seemed very quiet but there must be someone who would take her in.

The canvases along the walls at the other end of the room were a blur of colour from where she sat, getting only a slanting view, and she had taken a couple of steps towards them when she checked herself.

He had long legs, he wouldn't be away long, and somehow she didn't want him catching her examining his work. She couldn't have said why not. Curiosity was natural enough, but she didn't want to show any particular interest in him. It might be like reading his diary and she went back to the table and ate another sliver of cheese. She left the wine that remained in her glass alone, although she was sober again now.

Rafe was back within minutes with a medium-sized case and a haversack. 'Which one?' he asked.

'They're in the case.'

He put it on the table, pushing dishes to one side, and she undid the strap and turned the small key in the locks. From an envelope near the top she took a photograph of a pretty girl and a tall young man in army sergeant's uniform. The girl was her grandmother, wearing what must have been a smart suit in the forties, and a little pillbox hat on upswept hair.

It was a studio photograph, slightly faded. Caroline said, 'He came home once. That's when they were married and that's when he told her all I know.'

A black and white pencil head and shoulders sketch fell from the envelope and she explained, 'That was in her papers. It's him.' There was a rough outline of mountains as a background, and Rafe picked it up, almost as if he recognised it, which was impossible, of course.

He said, 'Well, the car can go no further. This is the end of anything you'd call a road. From here even in the summer it's on mule or on foot, and at this time of year not even the locals are going far. We've already had some snow and there's more on the way. Are you sure you want to go up?'

That was why she had come. She said, 'They lived up there, didn't they?'

'Yes, but——' He looked her up and down and the slow glance spoke louder than words. She knew how she looked and she could only repeat doggedly.

'Yes, I want to go.'

'We'll turn back when you've had enough.'

That was what any sensible guide would say. But she

did wish he would stop harping on her not getting far because he was really getting on her nerves.

'It's too late to set off today,' he said. 'We'll leave in the morning. You can have the loft tonight. It's rough but it's as good as you'll get.'

Up the wooden ladder into the dark hole in the ceiling probably *was* as good as she would be offered anywhere, but, 'Where will you sleep?' she asked.

'Down here. On there.' There seemed to be a wide ledge running along the wall this end of the room, and she blinked at it. 'That's where families sleep,' he told her, and she grinned wryly.

'I've heard of being past your shelf date—my father's got a grocer's shop—but this is something else.'

'Hardly Virginia Grove, is it?' He was laughing at her, and she almost said, No, but then you're hardly Christopher, are you? She held that back because it wouldn't have embarrassed him, it would have amused him.

'Now I'll take you to meet somebody,' he said. 'Put your coat on and bring the sketch.'

Without a word she got into coat, scarf and gloves. She wouldn't have gone strolling out without wrapping herself up, although he had, but she didn't say that either. Tomorrow he was taking her into the mountains where she would jump if he said jump, so she had better start co-operating and not getting riled.

She picked up the sketch and followed him out of the house into the bitter cold. She could smell the snow. After the warmth the icy air made her eyes water and when she breathed it was like pepper in her nostrils. The white-capped mountains were dappled with snow, some of the slopes were wooded and she looked up at what seemed to be a huddle of buildings on one of the ranges high above.

Beside her Rafe said, 'Half of them have gone from this village for the winter. That's completely deserted.'

A ghost hamlet. She could believe that. She had thought the same about this place when she came into it but there were people around now, black-clad women in doorways, moustachioed men in boots and breeches standing in small groups. All of them, it seemed to Caroline, looking her way.

Some called across to Rafe and he answered. What he had to say appeared to satisfy them because he got nods and smiles in reply, and she asked, 'What are you saying?'

'You don't speak Greek?'

'Only the odd tourist phrase.'

He said drily, 'When you were planning this exercise I'd have thought you'd have started by learning more than the odd phrase.'

'I didn't exactly plan it.' She was staring at the mountains, not at him. 'I suddenly felt that I had to come.'

'Why?'

Because it had seemed like her last chance. She shrugged, still looking up at the craggy peaks that towered on three sides of the village, and he said, 'You won't find Shangri-la up there.'

'What? Oh!' But *Lost Horizon* was set in the mountains of Tibet and it was a story. She said, 'I'm not seraching for paradise; I've got everything I need for a happy life.'

'With Christopher?' The mockery in his voice made her seethe. Here he was, living rougher than rough and looking it, and still sneering at Christopher.

The path was cobbled and uneven and when she stepped on a broken stone and almost lurched against him she stopped staring skywards and watched where she was going instead. He was her guide and nothing else. She would not let him goad her into a slanging match.

They passed another doorway and another woman who said a few words; Rafe replied and the woman smiled, and Caroline asked, 'What *are* you telling them?'

'You should have learned the language—I could be saying anything.'

She wouldn't put it past him, but he couldn't be saying anything too awful because they were all looking approving. 'Well?' she persisted.

'I'm telling them that you're my brother's wife-to-be and therefore my sister.'

'That's all right, then, is it?'

'They're great family folk. They'd expect me to be your chaperon and protector.'

'Thank you,' she said stiffly, resisting the urge to stress, You are my guide and that's all I need. Besides, how could she be his sister when Christopher would not have acknowledged him as a brother? She asked, 'Who are we going to talk to?'

'I'll be talking to him as you can't,' he said cheerfully. 'Uncle Giorgio was with the Resistance in the White Mountains, so he should remember your grandfather,' and when she thanked him this time she meant it.

There were more people in the square now, and alongside the church they walked down another cobbled alley, skirting the boulders, reaching a single-storey house with a heavy wooden door slightly ajar.

Rafe pushed the door further and called, and it was

opened by a man who greeted him and gave Caroline a welcoming smile when Rafe introduced her, then stood aside, motioning them both inside.

The light seemed dim in here and the room full. Two women were at a table preparing food, and there were children around. A middle-aged man had opened the door and an elderly man sat by what was probably a charcoal fire.

Caroline couldn't follow what Rafe was saying until he said her grandfather's name, Daniel Hammond, and then the old woman put down a knife with which she was chopping herbs and crossed herself, murmuring a prayer, and the old man got up from his chair and looked at Caroline as if she were his own long lost granddaughter.

Rafe showed him the sketch and the old woman scurried to fetch another. The same artist, with mountain peaks behind the head and shoulders study. But this was Giorgio, with a shock of dark hair and a jaunty moustache, the eyes clear and bright. The young eagle was an old eagle now, and the hair that showed beneath the black-fringed turban was snow-white, but the eyes were as fierce as ever.

'Danni,' he said, 'fine boy,' and her eyes swam with sudden tears. She could have hugged the old patriarch but he had such tremendous dignity that she could only swallow the lump in her throat and say,

'This is wonderful,' to Rafe. 'Please tell him it's wonderful.'

She should have learned some of the language before she came. She could have done. Her French was fairly fluent, and when she went back home she would start to learn Greek. For her own pleasure, not because she was likely to be coming this way again.

If she couldn't understand the words she could still feel the warmth of her welcome in this household. Giorgio was talking, the women were smiling and talking, and now Giorgio was issuing orders to the younger man, who grinned as he turned to go, and Caroline plucked at Rafe's sleeve and asked, 'What's happening.'

'Pavlos is off to tell their friends that Danni's grand-daughter is here.'

She hadn't expected this. She had thought she would be lucky if she found anyone who remembered. She said, 'But it was so long ago.'

'Not to them,' said Rafe.

If half the villagers had left for winter quarters nearer the foothills, all those who remained must have followed Pavlos back to this house, because now the room *was* full, and a chattering crowd spilled out on to the road.

Three old men had formed an inner circle with Giorgio, Rafe and Caroline, and she didn't need telling that they had been Danni's comrades. Rafe told her their names, that one had been a runner, carrying messages over the mountains from cave to cave, another had been a wireless station guard. They could have been hardly more than boys during those perilous times, and they passed the photograph and the sketch of the young man who was her grandfather from one to the other as if they remembered him well.

They wanted to know if Danni had had a son who he had never seen, and she told them, through Rafe, that that was her father, but no, he was not with her. She was here alone. Next time perhaps.

There had been no question of her father coming with her. He wouldn't have seen the point of it. He was a kind man, proud of his daughter who would be marrying a Drayford and living in the big house. But beyond that he had no imagination at all. There was nothing to bring him here. He was Danni's son but the zest for adventure had missed him.

She thought Rafe looked thoughtful briefly when she said that about 'next time', and she wondered if he might ask her later why her father had shown no interest in her search for their roots.

Then the gathering began to shift. They had all been milling around getting a glimpse of Caroline, but now they were on the move. Giorgio and his friends were on their feet and Rafe was guiding Caroline, who asked, 'Where are we going?'

'You're a celebrity, a VIP,' he told her. 'There hasn't been a wedding since the summer and their saint's day isn't for another three months, so you're a good excuse for a party.'

She had never been a star attraction before. She had compered fashion shows and helped Mrs Drayford hostessing a few times at Virginia Grove, but this was a much more personal and touching kind of tribute.

'I thought I was having a party,' she said, and Rafe laughed.

'You've seen nothing yet.'

A building near the church was a school but by the time Caroline walked in benches and tables had been moved and a party atmosphere had taken over.

Food and drink were filling the tables. The villagers came carrying bottles and jugs, and bowls and dishes piled high, set them down and hurried to where Caroline was seated, to smile at her and say they were happy and she was welcome.

At least she knew 'thank you' in Greek. She said it

again and again. The older women blessed her, she could follow that. Some of them had a little English, and the grizzled old partisans sat around her like a guard of honour.

She was queen for the day, a gypsy princess. Almost at once a man was plucking on a three-stringed lyre and another was playing a lute to the rhythm of stamping, dancing feet. Songs were sung, and one long dramatic poem was recited.

Caroline was fond of poetry and, although she couldn't understand the language of this one, the cadence moved her like a strange and stirring music.

Rafe stayed with her, translating sometimes, sometimes saying, 'Later,' although she was always desperate to know what the words meant. Because the old partisans were recalling long-ago exploits, capping each other's stories and roaring with laughter. Then shaking their heads, grim-faced, over the dark days of grief and terror.

But it was mostly celebration, and as the wine flowed the tempo of the dancing quickened until the ground seemed to shake under the pounding feet, and Caroline could have sworn that the old men and women grew young again. She could see the Giorgio of the sketch in the wrinkled visage of the proud old man, until he seemed no older than Rafe. And Rafe could well have been one of his comrades in arms.

Rafe Drayford would have made a good mountain fighter. He had the physical power, the sinewy athleticism, the keen dark eyes, and the dangerous edge to him even now while he was lounging and laughing.

Some of these men were armed; she saw knives in belts and there were guns around. She thought Rafe was not, but with him she was not sure, and nobody coming in here would have fingered him as an outsider. She was the pale-skinned English rose, but because of the name she bore she was an honoured guest.

She drank a fiery white liqueur and ate olives and walnuts, and when Rafe refilled her glass she wondered if he was hoping she would have a hangover in the morning which would make mountaineering seem less attractive. She had to be in top form, refreshed and clear-headed, and after that she stayed with the food and steered clear of the wine.

The food was a feast and she tried most of the dishes, taking a little of everything because she wanted to remember it all, down to the fillings in the little potatoes that were baked in their skins, and the combinations of salads.

Just for herself. When she got home if she told anyone about this it would be like tourist talk to them because nobody would understand what it had meant to her. Anna Drayford was only interested in Rafe, and her parents' concern had been that she was taking a holiday without Christopher. They wouldn't have her offend him for the world, and if he had been prepared to come with her she would have brought him.

She was glad now that she hadn't because this was a million miles from Christopher's scene. Rafe would have sent him into a black mood for a start. He might have enjoyed seeing the conditions Rafe was living in—that would have proved his point that his brother was a ne'er-do-well—but the force of personality that Christopher resented in his brother was stronger than ever.

Rafe would have looked at him with that contemptuous half-smile and Christopher would have got away as fast as the hired car would take him. He certainly

wouldn't have let Caroline stay for the party. They had
had some lovely party evenings at Virginia Grove, and
she had gone with him to what had seemed very lively
affairs. But this beat them all.

She leaned forward, watching the dancers, and when
several shots rang out she jerked back, turning to Rafe.
'Just high spirits,' he said.

'They're *shooting*.'

'Only into the rafters.'

It hushed the music and stilled the dancers for a
moment, and the priest, who had been drinking with
the elders, got up and wagged an admonishing finger,
smiling benevolently, not seeing much wrong with this
but hushing them, for now at least.

No, Caroline thought, Christopher would not be
enjoying himself here. Christopher would have dived
under the table at that.

But she was enjoying herself. It was mainly the men
who were dancing. And shooting. Rather a macho
society, this. But the girls were joining in the dancing
here and there. She saw Elpida, who knew all the steps
and was as graceful as a professional. She danced for a
while then she came across to them and said something
to Rafe, her dark eyes flicking over Caroline.

He translated, 'She says my sister-to-be, Danni's
granddaughter, is welcome.'

'Thank you,' Caroline murmured again, and Elpida
said something else, as an aside to Rafe.

'And?' Caroline prompted.

'And,' he said solemnly, 'you look very pale; perhaps
my brother should take better care of you.'

She was naturally pale. Christopher loved her fair
skin. He called her his lily-girl.

'Tell her,' said Caroline, 'that my fiancé takes very good care of me, in every possible way.'

'Does he, now?' drawled Rafe, and for some idiotic reason she blushed to the roots of her hair and was glad that Elpida was holding Rafe's hand and urging him into the dance with her. 'Excuse me,' he said to Caroline.

'Any time,' she said blithely. 'This I must see.'

The dance steps were complicated but he seemed to move through them as easily as the other men. There had to be better dancers, and this was a good looking race, but Rafe Drayford and Elpida were a strikingly handsome pair. Caroline was not the only one watching them. One young man she saw followed them so closely that she thought he must have a soft spot for Elpida, especially when she saw him sigh before he turned away.

She wondered if he would be letting off steam by firing a pistol into the rafters before the evening was through. It must be hard on the roof. Perhaps they all went up there after a party and slapped mud on the holes.

When Rafe came back, to sit down beside her again, Elpida shook her head and drifted off into the company, and Caroline asked, 'Who is the young man with the green and purple sash? He watched you.'

'He'd be watching Elpida.' Rafe poured himself more wine and held the bottle towards her. She put a hand on the top of her glass and said,

'They're quick on the trigger round here; I hope your intentions are honourable.'

'You've got sharp eyes.' He smiled like a tiger. 'But keep your pretty little nose out of my business. You may be family but advice from family I can do without.'

'Of course you can. Why change the habit of a lifetime?'

'Anyhow,' he said, 'it's time we were going. We have to make an early start in the morning.'

She was reluctant to leave. It was probable that never again would she be fêted like this, or feel such a bonding with so many people.

But time had flown by. Lamps had been lit. It was dark outside the windows and Rafe was right, they should be setting off at first light. She asked, 'Do you think I could have a dance before I go?'

He hesitated for a moment, then said, 'Why not?' and stood up to take her hand and lead her into the dancers.

She knew none of the steps, although she had been watching closely, but it wasn't that hard to follow because Rafe guided her, turning her where she should be facing, holding her when she should twirl.

She had never been an exhibitionist. She was good at a number of things apart from her job, but she had acquired her accomplishments quietly. Learning to swim, she had never jumped in at the deep end and splashed her way to the side, although now she could out-swim almost everyone she knew.

Back home she was a good dancer but she would not have been stumbling and laughing like this, needing her partner to keep her from skipping the wrong way. As they danced faster she was getting the knack, although it wouldn't matter if she didn't because it was fun, and when the musicians paused to take a long drink she looked up into the dark face of the man beside her and said, 'Thank you. If you're as good a guide in the mountains I'll be all right.'

Rafe laughed at that. 'I'd better be better. I'm not

much of a dancer and we won't be doing any capering up there.'

He was humouring her; he thought she was high. She was, but it was not the wine or the exertion that had brought the colour into her cheeks. It was finding herself in Rafe Drayford's hands. He had been the spice of danger in the dance, and it was high time they called it a day, although the party showed no sign of winding down.

Outside the cold came at her again. She had wrapped her scarf over her head and shoulders and dug her gloved hands deep into her pockets as she walked beside Rafe, across the square towards the alley and his house.

She stopped once to look up again in the direction of the deserted hamlet. She thought it glittered in the moonlight but it might have been snow on a ridge she was seeing, although he followed her glance and said, 'They sheltered the partisans.'

'I'd like to get up there.'

'If you do I'll go home for your wedding.' He meant that there was no chance of that, and she drawled,

'You're on,' for no reason except that she seemed unable to resist a challenge that came from him.

As he opened the door a lamp threw a mellow glow, filling the long room with shadows. The lamp was on the table in the kitchen, and Elpida got up from a chair by the table and came to meet them. Her attitude was that of the woman of the house who had been landed with a lodger she could do without. Her smile was twitchy and when Rafe spoke to her he sounded amused.

'Look.' Caroline began. She had been going to say, Can't somebody else take me in? But he had picked up

her case and her haversack and was carting them up
into the attic. She said, 'Sorry,' to Elpida, who said,

'Brother's wife,' as if she needed reassuring on that.

'Soon,' said Caroline.

Rafe was back at once, telling her what she could
see—'The ablutions aren't quite what you're used to.'

There was a stone sink and a bucket of water,
adequate for washing but not all she needed. She
asked, 'Where's the loo. . .the privvy?' and prayed,
Please not the bucket!

He produced a hefty torch and opened the door,
casting light into the darkness. 'Out there. Don't fall
in.'

She didn't want him taking her and she felt that
Elpida might have pushed her in. 'I'll find it,' she said
hastily.

She thought she did. She got out of the house and in
again as quickly as possible, and asked, 'May I use
some water from the bucket?'

'Of course.'

She poured a little into a bowl, dabbed her hands
and face and dried them on a very rough towel. All the
time she could feel Elpida glowering and wondered
whether she should be offering to take the shelf and
leave them whatever kind of bed it was under the
eaves.

The heck, she thought; he offered. And I don't think
I could sleep on a shelf and I'm surely getting enough
new experiences without that.

She gave her hands a final rub and asked Rafe,
'What time in the morning?' It was past midnight now
by her watch. The day had passed so quickly.

He said, 'Seven o'clock? You have boots, suitable
clothing?'

She had packed for where she wanted to go. 'Yes.'

'Goodnight, then.' He smiled, but Elpida was unsmiling, and Caroline couldn't resist,

'Don't fall off the ledge.'

'If I do,' he said, 'you'll be the first to know.'

Surely not, she thought. Surely Elpida would notice. But that could be making mischief if Elpida got the drift of it so she bade them both goodnight, and climbed the rickety ladder, emerging head and shoulders into the attic and hauling herself up to look around.

He had brought a lamp up while she was outside. It stood on a battered tin trunk, which seemed to be all the furniture there was, except for a chair and an old-fashioned army camp-bed, a cumbersome affair of wooden struts and webbing.

With a narrow slit of a window and the roof sloping down it was claustrophobic up here, but she had to allow the two below some privacy and she closed the heavy trapdoor. It shut with a thump and she hoped she could lift it again without breaking every fingernail.

She had always been proud of her hands. So was Christopher. When he had put on the ruby ring he'd said, 'Your hands are so beautiful. My mother says you can always tell a lady by her hands.'

She had thought that funny at the time, but a compliment and rather sweet. If she did wreck her prettily manicured nails she would have to invest in a few falsies before she presented herself again for inspection at Virginia Grove.

An opening led to an empty room, even smaller than this, and then she tried the bed, which was as spartan as she'd feared. A thin mattress seemed to be stuffed with straw and so did a pillow that was hardly thicker than a mat. There were two heavy blankets and that was it.

She didn't complain. Nobody had expected her and it was a bed for the night. Like camping out, although she hadn't done that since she was a child on occasional holidays with schoolfriends and their parents. In warmer circumstances. She couldn't complain and she couldn't undress either. She would need to stay wrapped up to keep warm enough to sleep.

She opened her case and took out the boots she would be wearing tomorrow, doing no other unpacking, as there was nowhere to put anything except over the chair. She wrapped the rough pillow in her nightshirt—at least there would be something smooth against her face—and then she turned out the lamp and climbed carefully into bed. It looked solid but it might wobble; it was old enough to have deathwatch beetles in the woodwork.

Everything was silent. They could still be dancing—and maybe shooting—at the party, but these walls were thick and the only window was hardly wider than a slit. She could hear nothing. Downstairs they were either talking softly or not talking at all, and she was surprised that the thought of Rafe and Elpida not talking should disturb her.

The picture flashed into her mind of how he would look shirtless, the rippling muscles of the broad back, taking Elpida into his arms; and she shook her head sharply, clearing that image before her imagination really ran riot.

She would think about the party. There was so much to remember, but Rafe Drayford was with her through all of it. His presence was so powerful that she had been conscious of him every minute since she had walked into this house.

When he was dancing with Elpida she had thought what a striking couple they were. She and Christopher looked good together. She knew that and she had been told that, but beside Rafe and Elpida they would be like shadows. Compared with Rafe Christopher was——

She stopped right there. Christopher was no shadow. He was different from Rafe and he was the better man. Rafe Drayford had made a strong impression on her but that didn't mean that she liked him. He was not likeable. He was a womaniser who had walked out on the girl called Isabel, and there must have been others before Elpida. He was a thief who had robbed his father. He was not to be trusted and, although he would be a good guide, she was sure, when she once was home she hoped she would never have to see him again.

She couldn't see much through the narrow slit of window and only a little light streamed in, but she could sense the vastness of the mountain ranges, rising so high around this village that they blotted out the sky.

She felt small and vulnerable, and Rafe was right— she wouldn't get far by the standards of mountain folk. But it would be something to climb just high enough to be able to imagine how it might have been, hiding out, looking down on a village with your wireless station in a safer higher place, in a cave among the rocks and ravines. As Danni must have done.

Rafe had sounded as if you would need to be a mountain goat to get to the Cave of the Winds, and there wasn't much chance that she would reach the deserted hamlet. She would surprise herself if she did, and she would astonish Rafe, maybe even knocking the sneer off his face.

He didn't believe she had a hope or he wouldn't have said that about returning for the wedding if she did, because he had no intention of going home to Virginia Grove. Not now. Not ever, she thought. And he had reasons for keeping away.

The girl he'd left behind was surely well over him by now. Nobody talked about her in front of Caroline but it had been nearly five years. There was the money, of course, quite a lot of money. His mother had said he would be welcomed if he met his father halfway, so what did that mean? Apologise? Pay back half the cash?

He couldn't have any cash or he wouldn't be living like this, and he wasn't a man for backing down, but his mother would probably be glad to see him again. His brother would not. Christopher would rather Rafe were dead.

She had been drifting into sleep, in spite of the hardness of the bed. Just before you blacked out your mind could come up with something that you had never consciously considered. That happened to Caroline. A suspicion that Christopher would rather his brother were dead.

But that was a dreadful thought. It shocked her awake again, whispering, '*No. . .*' as if she had said it aloud. Christopher would rather his brother stayed away; that didn't mean he wanted him dead. She tried to laugh at herself, although it hadn't been funny, just crazy.

Rafe would not be turning up for the wedding but he would certainly create a stir if he did. She could imagine a Drayford gathering and Rafe striding in, looking the way he did now. She could imagine them either frozen rigid or running for cover—'cat among the pigeons' wouldn't be near it. Which side of the church would they put him in? Friend of the bride's? He certainly was no friend of the groom's. Please keep a seat for my mountain man, she would have to say.

She was smiling now. That zany scenario had cheered her up because he was not going home and all she had to worry about was climbing her mountain.

She turned her head into the pillow, against the nightshirt she had wrapped around it, and a spike of corn pierced the cover, scratching her cheek quite painfully.

That had *hurt*. 'Elpida doesn't have your delicacy,' Rafe had said. 'This wouldn't scar her.' He had meant his unshaven face, and that could have something in common with prickly straw.

She folded the nightshirt into a thick scarf and wrapped it around her head, using her arm as a pillow, feeling almost as resentful and irritated as if she had scratched her cheek against Rafe Drayford's face.

# CHAPTER THREE

CAROLINE woke to a banging noise and struggled to sit up, still bleary although she was not usually such a sound sleeper. It took a few seconds for her to realise where she was and that knocking was coming from the trapdoor. 'Yes?' she called, and the trapdoor lifted.

'Coffee?' said Rafe, holding the door up. Good lord, she thought, room service!

By daylight the room was even more rugged than it had seemed last night. He had shaved but it hadn't improved him much. The thick dark curling hair behind his ears was still unruly and the navy blue shirt he wore was probably the one he had been wearing yesterday.

She must look odd herself, with a nightshirt wrapped around her head like an outsize turban, and fully dressed under the blankets. She lifted the blankets off her legs and they were so heavy that it was no wonder she had slept deeply. Last night she had wriggled down under them, and they must have lain on her as a dead weight till morning.

When he came up, carrying a steaming mug, immediately the little room seemed smaller, as if the roof was coming down and the walls were closing in. He invaded her space. That was one of the things she had against him and she thought crazily, I should think a mountain will be big enough for both of us.

She took the mug and muttered her thanks. 'You slept well?' he asked.

'I must have.' She couldn't have done much tossing

under those blankets. She had gone out like a light, she knew, and she had a vague memory of dreams that she couldn't pin down. Her head was still spinning and she needed this coffee. She sat on the side of the camp-bed, sipping, and he picked up the boots she had taken out of her case.

'Good,' he said. She took the mug away from her lips to say, You approve? How lovely, but she mustn't get off to a bad start by being uppity this early, although when he asked, 'What else?' she snapped.

'Maybe you'd like to unpack for me.'

He grinned. 'That's carrying room service too far,' and with anyone else she would have smiled and said, Funny, I was thinking the coffee was super room service. 'But I would like to see what you call suitable clothing,' he said.

She put her mug down, and got up and opened the lid of her case and started piling the contents on the bed. She was sure he expected her to have brought clothes that might be suitable for a tourist and that he could be superior about.

She knew what the weather conditions were likely to be and she had spent extravagantly in a specialist store. Her parents would have been appalled at the cost for one short holiday, and even Christopher would have been taken aback, but she was spending her own savings and she had the protective clothing if not the expertise for going up a mountain—thermal under-wear, including long mountain-climbing socks, sweaters, tough gloves, fleeced hooded jacket, waterproofed trouses and woollen cap.

He nodded over that lot. 'Fine. What's in the haversack?'

'Feel free,' she said, and tossed it over to him. 'While

you're doing a kit inspection you might as well see the lot.' There were only towels and toiletries, a first-aid kit, paperback novel and a guidebook on Crete. 'Now,' she said, 'can I get changed?'

It was cold, stripping off for even a few seconds. She dragged the thicker, warmer clothing on as fast as possible, and then finished drinking her coffee.

She was anxious to get out of this house. Yesterday had been wonderful. For the rest of her life she would remember the old partisans and how the memory of her grandfather was still alive here. She was grateful that Mrs Drayford's letter had brought her to this village and that Christopher's brother saw himself as her protector and would take her safely into the mountains.

So, be thankful, she scolded herself, and stop feeling that he's stopping you breathing. When you're out of the house it will be better.

She had to be careful, going down the ladder in her heavier shoes. It would have been very ironic if she'd sprained an ankle before she started, and she took each rung slowly, planting her foot firmly before she felt for the next.

Rafe was near. She didn't look for him but she could sense him at the table, an arm's stretch from the ladder, and then she thought that he might come and lift her down and she didn't want that, so she got down the last three rungs faster.

When she looked around there was no sign of Elpida. She must have left either very late or very early. She was not seeing them off and she might not be overjoyed about Rafe spending the day with Caroline.

It wouldn't have surprised Caroline if Elpida had been coming with them. She would know the mountains better than Rafe did. She would be able to cover the crags and the crevices with the sure-footedness she had shown on the dance-floor last night. Beside her Caroline would have the grace of a sack of potatoes. On the whole, even if Elpida was a born guide, Caroline would rather she stayed at home.

Rafe was wearing a black leather jacket and pouring what looked like a jug of yoghurt into what looked like a bowl of porridge. 'Eat this,' he said.

'Must I?' She wasn't hungry after all she'd eaten yesterday.

'Yes.' He pushed a jar of honey towards her and she dug a spoonful out, stirring it slowly into the mixture.

It was quite palatable, not worth arguing over—energising probably, and she was going to need energy.

He had taken a chair opposite, watching her, and she almost put down her spoon and flung out both hands as if she could push him away, although the table was between them.

Then he said, 'Have you had any mountaineering experience?'

'No.'

'Not even taken a course?'

'No, but neither had my grandfather.' She found herself chattering nervously. 'I think his mother was Welsh. Maybe he climbed Welsh mountains when he was a boy; I don't really know.'

'I have a suggestion,' said Rafe. 'I can tell you about the Resistance; Giorgio and his friends have talked to me. Why don't you settle for walking to the limits of the village, the summer grazing ground, rather than going up into the mountains?'

She said stubbornly, 'I want to climb a mountain.'

'In the winter?' He had asked her that before. Now

he was making a final appeal to her common sense, and she answered again,

'Yes. Now.'

She was sounding petulant, although she was trying to give an impression of calm decisiveness. After a moment he said, 'Elpida's right. My brother should take better care of you. He should not have let you come here.'

'What do you mean, let me?' she shrilled. 'Christopher doesn't give me orders.' Now she was sounding like a virago, which was the last thing in the world she was, but Rafe Drayford managed to irritate her right out of character. And he was grinning.

'Of course he doesn't, he's much too civilised.' He went on smiling although she knew he was in earnest. 'Well, if I'm taking you up there I'm giving the orders. I don't want you breaking your neck—I'd prefer it if you didn't even break a leg. And although you seem to have suitable gear, physically and emotionally I think you are quite unprepared.'

She didn't think so. She thought she might have resources that had never been called on before. Or it could be the antagonism she felt for him that was stiffening her spine and charging her whole nervous system like an adrenalin shot.

She said sulkily, 'And if I say that I couldn't care less what you think I suppose you opt out and I either find another guide or go up on my own.'

That stopped him smiling. 'My God,' he said. 'You're not just unprepared, you're deranged. You'd start a landslide in under ten minutes and bury yourself.'

She wouldn't dream of wandering off alone but he seemed to think she was that irresponsible because he said, 'Oh, I'll take you. But I'm telling you that if you don't do exactly as you're told I'll bring you back, probably slung over my shoulder.'

'Thank you.' For a few sweet seconds she had annoyed him, and devilry led her on to add, 'I shall tell Christopher how helpful you've been.'

The shuttered look that came into his eyes was so fleeting that she couldn't have sworn she'd seen it before he laughed. 'Tell my mother to keep writing to me,' he said. 'I'll be interested to hear how you and Christopher get along.'

They had never had a cross word. The nearest they had come to a disagreement was over her trip to Crete and she was sure that when she got back Christopher would be waiting, and if he had been hurt by her going off on her own his reproof would be mild. There would be no quarrel. She said, 'We get along marvellously.'

'So far,' said Rafe. 'But in about twelve months' time you could give them all something to think about.'

'What do you mean?'

'Well, I don't mean grandchildren.'

That was crassly offensive but her instinctive response was almost as uncouth. She was so close to hurling the bowl and what was left of the contents into his face that she had lifted it off the table before she realised what was happening to her. Then she needed long enough to count to five slowly before she could say, sounding cool, 'I'll ask her to keep you posted.'

'I'll look forward to it. Finished, have you?'

She presumed he meant the porridge in the bowl she was still holding and she put it down. 'Yes, I've finished.'

'Then let's go.'

'What do I take with me?'

'Nothing.' There was a large backpack on the floor
that looked well filled. 'I'd prefer you to travel light.'

That would make it easier for her, of course. She
picked up her shoulder bag—she had hung it by the
strap on the back of the chair—and explained, 'I've got
my passport, money and tickets in this.'

'You won't need them where we're going. I'll leave
it next door for you.'

She handed it over and as soon as he closed the
street door behind him she found herself actually
looking around for something she could throw against
the wall. The odd cooking pot might have made a
satisfying clatter, but that would be admitting she had
lost her self-control and she had not and she would
not.

Until now she couldn't remember ever losing her
temper. Not to the stage of flying into a red-hot rage.
She sometimes met people who irritated her—who
didn't? But these vibes were savage and this should
make her feel closer to Christopher. He couldn't stand
the sight of his brother and she had never met anybody
before who made her want to scream.

He was gone for almost ten minutes. When she
opened the front door he was almost at it and, although
this was unreasonable, she was as disgruntled as if she
had expected to be alone and he was intruding.

He was the only sign of life in this little alley. The
village was as quiet as it had seemed yesterday when
she had arrived here. She knew now that some families
were braving the winter out in some of the shuttered
houses, but doors were closed and the little square was
empty.

They passed her car and came to the church where
she had lit a candle, and she asked, 'Can I go in?'

'It's open,' he said. 'Although I don't know if Father John will be on duty yet after last night.'

'I lit a candle here yesterday. The icon was a woman.'

'Ayia Anna, the mother of Mary.'

'She was pouring water from some sort of vessel.'

'Representing chastity and purity.'

'Well, I think I should thank her. I asked for help and she sent me a guide.'

'Don't thank her yet,' he said. 'She isn't in the tourist business. Chastity, purity and fertility. The women here ask her for a strong, healthy child.'

'Oh!' she said. 'Well, that can't be bad.'

He opened the church door for her and there seemed to be fewer candles burning this morning. Hers had long guttered out but one still burned in the alcove of the Virgin's mother. 'Try St George,' said Rafe. 'He was a warrior. Third from the left on the other side of the altar.'

He didn't go in himself but Caroline did, and she prayed again, kneeling on the cold stones. A prayer for the men and women who had died in that bitter struggle, as Giorgio's wife had prayed for Danni when she heard his name.

Then she looked for St George, and found him in a wall-painting, a row of almost identical men, all in robes and haloes. He was the one with the sword, and, while they all looked sombre, she thought he was the most forbidding of the lot.

Outside, Rafe asked, 'Did you find him?'

She said, 'You light him a candle. I don't think he approved of me.' He laughed at that and she felt he was laughing at her.

Behind one of the houses they began to climb, going up a dirt track into the summer grazing lands. Only a few sheep and goats remained, the goat-bells tinkling in the clear cold air, and she could hear her own regular breathing as she kept up a steady climbing pace a couple of steps behind the man.

Over his shoulder he told her, 'I'm taking you on the track the locals use. It's not easy to find even in summer. Obviously it's harder now but it's the only way you'll manage any sort of climb.'

He was talking sense, so why should that make her want to screech, How do you know? I could be a natural climber. I might be able to race you to the top.

She couldn't say that of course, but she glared at his backpack and the back of his head as she murmured, 'Handy you knowing the way. How long have you been here?'

'Nearly three years, on and off.'

This must be his nearest to a permanent address, although as far as she knew it was the first time he had written to his mother from here. 'Where else?' she enquired and got reminded,

'It's your grandfather's stamping ground we're covering, not mine.'

She had absolutely no interest in where he had been and she said, 'Just making conversation,' through clenched teeth.

'Save your breath,' he advised her, 'you're going to need it.'

She didn't want to talk to him. She wished she could block him out of her sight and her mind, but as that was impossible the next best thing was silence.

The silence and the incredible vastness of the mountains were like another planet to a girl who had never known physical loneliness before. It was terrifying and glorious, and almost at once the going was tough.

The air was ice-cold but she was warm in her insulated suit, scrambling over the rocks. Even in summer she wouldn't have thought there was much pasture up here. It seemed mostly rocks and stunted shrubs and slithering scree underfoot. He was going slowly; she could keep up and she had known it would be an endurance test, but she hoped he would stop before she had to admit she needed to rest as she followed him doggedly and silently.

There were cypress and fir tree forests on some of the mountain ranges and, still climbing, Rafe said, 'They hid in the forests too, of course, and so did some of the wanted Cretans and their families.'

She nodded, which was stupid as he wasn't looking at her, and he turned his head sharply, then grinned. 'For a moment I thought you weren't here.'

'Where else would I be?'

They were well above the village now and he seemed to decide it was time he kept an eye on her because he began to walk alongside instead of letting her trail behind, and she asked, 'Where did you think I'd gone?'

'I didn't until you didn't answer. Then I had a nasty moment wondering if I'd lost you already.' He was smiling at her and she thought, Patronising git! She said,

'You told me to be quiet and save my breath.'

'So I did. It's nice to see you can take orders.'

'Only up mountains.'

'Where else would I be issuing them?' he said, and suddenly she was laughing too. It was the first time she had laughed with him, and the sound of their laughter seemed to be carried on the wind like the spirit of the mountains, wild and free. She was getting fanciful, imagining things, and she began to talk fast.

'They've told you about the Resistance? Please, tell me. Up here, they would have been up here?'

He told her, as they climbed, how men like her grandfather had lived in the White Mountains, never staying in one place long, sometimes burying their transmitter hastily, sometimes carrying it and the batteries on their backs in suitcases, as they moved from cave to cave, hideout to hideout.

Any of the caves could have been a lair. The mountains were riddled with them, hidden by rocks and undergrowth. Some of the caves were on precipices where only mountain goats and mountain men could reach them. But caves they passed would be like the caves from which Danni had sent and received messages, sometimes from crevices so small that a man would crouch in there alone, wireless operators like Danni.

She said, 'I want to go into a cave.'

'We can find you one, but you won't mind if I stay outside.'

If the cave was small she would rather go in alone, but she asked, 'What's the risk?'

'It's not so much a risk as a near cert you'll come out with more than you go in with. Vermin. Lice.'

'Ah!' She had not been prepared for that. 'Thanks for warning me.'

'Part of the service,' he said. 'You want to go on?'

'Of course.'

They stayed on the track. Most of the time Caroline couldn't see it at all, but he seemed to know where he was going and he kept her on it, climbing higher and higher, the rise getting steeper in a hazardous haul over rocks and crags. A razor-keen wind blew and the ice-covered ground was treacherous.

Her back and her legs were aching when she slipped. She had had several narrow escapes, where she had almost lost her balance and Rafe had grabbed her, but this time she went so suddenly that she was slithering down the mountainside almost before he could turn.

Straight for a boulder, which knocked the breath out of her and gave him the few seconds he needed to bound down after her. She gulped in air. 'Sorry about that.'

'Are you all right?'

'Absolutely.' She was still gulping and puffing, but her thick clothing had protected her and she hadn't fallen far. She staggered upright, leaning against the boulder, and she was fine.

'We get roped from here,' he said. He slipped off his backpack and was unbuckling a strap. 'I didn't think you'd get this far,' he said to her, and she told him,

'I don't want to be roped.'

'Don't be stupid.'

It *was* stupid. She couldn't explain why she had to stay free of him, even if the next time she took a wrong step she slid all the way down to the village. She said stubbornly, 'No, I'll be all right.'

He had a thin rope coil in his hands. 'This is just a safety measure.'

'I know. I just don't want to be tied.'

'We're not playing bondage games. What *do* you and Christopher get up to in the privacy of Virginia Grove?'

He was making her sound like an idiot and her face flamed, although that was so unlikely that she nearly burst out laughing. She heard herself drawl, 'Nothing your mother couldn't watch.'

'That should limit the action,' he said. 'But I can't risk you losing your footing up here.'

'I won't. I'll go so carefully.'

'You certainly will.' But he put the rope back, fastened the backpack and hoisted it on to his shoulders again. 'See that?' He pointed a little further up the slope. 'It's a shepherd's hut. We'll make for that and then we'll take a break.'

They had been climbing for hours and her tumble had shaken her. She said brightly, '*What* a good idea,' and when he raised an eyebrow she said, 'I'm not going light-headed but I could use a break.'

'Not for long, and it's only a wind barrier.'

'I didn't think it would be a taverna.'

'But we do have coffee.'

She gave a rapturous sigh. 'Ah, bliss.'

She didn't slip again because he took her arm before they moved on, and although he was wearing gloves and she had layers of clothing she imagined she could feel the separate pressure of his fingers. She said, 'I can manage,' but he said,

'Shut up,' and so she stumbled along, still climbing, heading for what looked like a pile of rocks.

That was more or less what it was, a shack made of stacked stones but a shelter from the wind, and she was glad to get inside and get his hands off her. He hadn't actually held her all the way to the shepherd's hut but he had shepherded her, never letting her get out of reach, and she was beginning to wonder if the mountain *was* big enough for both of them.

But she was glad of his coffee, which he poured from a stainless-steel container, and she was surprised how quickly it revived her. As they sat in this little manmade cave, which she hoped was less of a haven for crawlies than the earthen ones, looking out over the mountain-side, her aching limbs were already feeling easier.

She stretched her back, flexing her shoulders, and he said, 'All right?'

'Fine, and the coffee's wonderful.'

She could get quite cosy in here. The wind chill was beginning to burn in her cheeks, although she had lathered her face with protective cream this morning. She was warming up and she thought, I could fall asleep and it wouldn't be a bad idea. I couldn't freeze in the hut in this gear. If I was with anyone else I'd say, Would you mind if I closed my eyes for five minutes? But I could never go home and tell them I'd slept with Rafe Drayford.

A giggle rose in her throat and he asked, 'What's the joke?'

'I think the caffeine's gone to my head. I've never had a picnic up a mountain this high before.'

Sitting on the ground, side by side, just inside the open door space of the hut, they were almost on eye level, so that when she turned her head she found herself looking straight into his eyes.

His eyes were as dark as pitch, under heavy lids, and when his gaze locked with hers she had the strangest sensation of being drawn into rushing darkness. It was like an explosion in her mind, blowing her reason. She couldn't turn away and when he did and began to talk, his voice unhurried and calm, she sat very still and felt that she was reeling.

'Just over the fold of that hill,' he was saying, 'is one of the plains where the parachute drops were made. The partisans lit marker fires in a "V for victory" sign to guide the drops, but sometimes they blew off course. Once some of the villagers were out at night collecting snails for food and they got a consignment of leather boot soles and flour, which was riches.'

She listened, and smiled because it was that kind of story, and thought, He's dangerous, I know that. He's arrogant, he's probably cruel, he's everything Christopher says; and I've never met anyone like him before, but I neither like him nor trust him.

'We'd better be moving,' he said.

Outside the hut the wind was waiting for them and she pulled the hood on her jacket up over her wollen hat. 'We'll be down before dark,' he said.

'Down?'

They were more than halfway to the deserted village. She looked up at it, shading her eyes in the bright light, and he said wearily, 'Come back in the summer.'

'Can't you manage it?'

That was just about the silliest thing she could have said, and of course he didn't answer that. He said, 'What is it with you? It's an empty hamlet, less than a dozen houses, all of them empty.'

'You said they sheltered men like my grandfather.'

'So did most of the villages. That was harder to get at than most, so it was considered safer.'

Here was something else she couldn't explain; why that hamlet should have become her target. The rarified atmosphere up here was probably getting to her, making her obsessive, but if she could get nearer the peaks she would feel she had met the challenge of the mountains. And, in a way, the challenge of the man. He was so sure she couldn't do it.

Not as certain maybe as he had been before they set off. He'd said she'd got further than he'd expected, but she did not want to turn back yet. The rest and the coffee had helped, so that, standing out here now, she almost believed she was as good as new.

She said, 'I've got to get there if I possibly can.'

'For no good reason.'

'Except that I want to desperately. I know there's no good reason. I know you think I'm behaving stupidly.'

He considered that, then he said, 'You're not stupid, but stubborn, spoiled, with a one-track mind for getting what you want.'

She could hear him, in spite of the wind and through the cap and the hood covering her ears, but if she hadn't been able to hear a word she could still have guessed what he was saying by his expression.

It didn't bother her. The insults applied far more to him than they did to her. Her determination to get her own way had only come out over this trip to Crete. Until then she had been amenable and even tempered and ready to consider other people's points of view.

'How's your heart?' he asked, and she was not sure she was hearing that right, until he went on, 'The last stretch is the toughest. You can't be as fragile as you look but I'd like to check your pulse.'

She said hastily, 'I couldn't be fitter.' She pulled off a glove and shoved her sleeve above her wrist, put fingertips on the pulse point and counted aloud. The beat would be faster than usual, after hours of strenuous exercise, but it was steady, and she suspected that if she had let him do the holding and counting there would have been a highly irregular rhythm.

She put her glove on again before she got frostbite and pleaded, 'You'll take me?'

'If you're that set on it. You do realise we'll be up there for the night? I'm carrying a sleeping bag and there is shelter, but it will make last night's doss seem like luxury.'

She ought to be saying, Let's turn back; but she was as excited as if years of boring training were giving her the chance to go for Olympic gold. 'I won't mind,' she said eagerly.

'If you flake out on the way I'll bed you down in a cave.'

She said, 'I won't.'

She let him fasten the rope round her waist without protesting. She hadn't wanted to be tied to him, any more than she had wanted him holding her arm to make sure she didn't slip, but from now on the way was going to be riskier than ever and she would do exactly what she was told, making no mistakes she could avoid.

She realised her first mistake within minutes: the idea that a short break and a few gulps of coffee could restore her like a good night's rest. Of course they couldn't. As she took the first steep bend on the winding road she was aching again, and with anyone else she would have agreed, You're right and I'm wrong; we should be turning back.

If he had paused soon and asked if she was sure about this, given her a chance to think again, she might have admitted defeat. But he didn't stop. There was no talking and she pushed on, head down into an ever keener wind.

Snow had fallen heavily up here; he must be following the contours of the ground, the shapes of rock formations. The snow was as hard as iron and that made the ascent slow and perilous, especially when they skirted sheer precipices where she was scrambling on hands and knees.

When the ground fell away and she saw how high she was she waited for sickness to strike her. She had never been scared of heights but she expected vertigo here and was surprised when it didn't come. Her grandfather must have had a head for heights—perhaps she had inherited it—and she had enough to worry about because after another couple of hours of this she would have crawled into a cave and shared it with vampire bats if it meant she could sleep.

She had never believed she could feel so weary that every bone and nerve was going numb. Sometimes Rafe hauled her, but most of the time she was dragging herself, step by step, inch by inch, and the weaker she felt the stronger the conviction grew that he was enjoying this.

He could have stopped her. He could have said no and she would have had to turn back, but she had asked and he had said, 'If you're that set on it,' and he must have been laughing then because he knew what it was like; and if she slipped over the edge and he had to yank her back on the path, that would make his day.

That would be a real bondage game, with her swinging on the end of a rope. If he fell she would do her damnedest to untie the knot and let him go, although if he fell he would take her with him—she couldn't be more than half his weight and she was none too steady up here. And he wouldn't fall. She was going in panicky jerks, while he was climbing with the easy movements of a born and practised athlete.

I hate you, she thought. If I get out of this alive I will poison you. His dark face always seemed close to hers, and she dared not shut her eyes tight because she had to see a little ahead. She had to keep going, although the only part of her that seemed to be working was her mind.

That was over-active, whirling away like crazy. Maybe hell was up not down, and she was clawing her

way up to hell, with her own personal attendant devil.
His dark eyebrows were white now, with a rime of
frost, and all her pain was his fault. Hate was the spur
that was keeping her going.

And she had no choice. There was shelter up there,
and it couldn't be much further. Meanwhile she had to
keep moving because if she dropped he would carry
her, and if he picked her up she would lose her last
scrap of sanity and go stark screaming mad.

Caroline had gone a little way before she realised
the ground was comparatively level. Until now it had
been mostly climbing, climbing, with sometimes a
couple of even steps and then up again. But this was
flat earth, a longer ledge.

'We're here,' Rafe said, and she blinked frost from
her eyelashes.

She really was in an appalling state. She would either
sleep for a week or never sleep again. She had reached
the very limits of her physical strength but the tension
in her mind had her strung up like a puppet on a string.

With anyone else she could have flopped down and
had a short burst of hysteria, laughed or cried, and let
the strain seep out of her. But not with him. She
managed to stay upright, and looked along the ledge at
the backs of several houses. Then she followed him
between them on to a small plateau and a few more
houses, perched a little higher.

Everything glittered white. Snow had covered it all.

'It's early winter yet,' he said. 'Two more months
and the snow will be over the roofs down here, covering
the doors up there, and there'll be no way in.'

'Hello hell,' she said.

'You could be right.'

There were still peaks towering above them,

although she felt as though she had scaled Everest. She asked, 'Where's the Cave of the Winds?'

'Higher, on the side of the canyon.'

'You've been there?'

'Yes.'

She said brightly, 'I must come in the summer; I must bring Christopher,' and knew that her mind was not connecting with her mouth. 'We'll both take a mountaineering course,' she babbled, and knew that Christopher would rather walk over burning coals and that she would never go mountain climbing again.

All of which Rafe understood perfectly. 'Stay here,' he said. 'I'll check the accommodation.'

She almost called after him, Order dinner and book me a hairdressing appointment, before she clamped her teeth on her lower lip. He would think she was hallucinating, dreaming up the mirage of a five-star hotel, and she couldn't have said 'I'm joking,' because she was not joking.

She was so close to hysteria, but would not show it in front of him. She was not having him slapping her face and shaking her back to sanity. She had never gone to pieces in her life—although she had never gone through such a horrendous day before.

But it was over for now. She could rest and get warm again. All she had to do now was walk a little further and say nothing, because her voice would come out thin and shrill and more than slightly crazy.

She watched him dully at first. He put his shoulder to a door and after a while it opened, so it wasn't locked although ice must have sealed it. All the houses looked alike, all closed and glittering white. Rafe came out of the first and tried another, and she shut her eyes then.

She couldn't remember why she had been hell-bent on getting up here. If she could have willed herself back into the village below, or home again, she wouldn't have hesitated for a moment. She should never have come to Crete. It had been a stupidly romantic impulse, and she was paying for it. A night on a bare mountain with a man she hadn't even got the strength to hate any more.

If she let herself speak–she would say, 'I hate you,' because the words were gagging in her throat, struggling to get out.

He was coming back for her and she went to meet him so that he wouldn't touch her. He turned as soon as she moved; he knew she would follow him, and she thought, I'm on automatic pilot. If I can operate like this until I'm rested I might be able to get down the mountain tomorrow.

It was as cold inside as out. This seemed more a barn than a house, Caroline thought; the table and chairs were of rough wood and there was no fuel in the blackened hearth. The walls kept the wind out but she could still feel it in her blood.

Rafe opened the backpack and took out a bedroll, which he unrolled and unzipped. 'Get into that,' he said.

It was surprisingly big, released from the backpack. She eased herself well into it and it wrapped around her. 'I'll look for some fuel,' he said. 'Meantime, take a slug of this.'

She took the hip flask and swallowed some brandy. It burned her throat and nearly made her sick, but she would have drunk the lot if she'd dared. Knocking herself out would have been one way of getting through the night. She had to hand it back after a few gulps but in her exhausted state it was enough to start warming her.

She saw him go and come back, carrying what she hoped was fuel. He offered her a square of chocolate and she knew that she would be sick if she ate that, but she got some soup down, and another cup of coffee, and when he held the brandy flask over that she nodded.

She was as warm as she was going to be and her body was asleep already. After she had drunk the coffee all her muscles below her neck went limp so that she could hardly have raised a finger.

Her mind was still racing and a dull ache throbbed in her temples, but she had to sleep, and before long the weariness took over and she lapsed into troubled slumber.

Perhaps, at first, her sleep was dreamless, but as soon as she was less deeply unconscious she was into a nightmare and back on the mountain.

She was climbing and struggling and always Rafe Drayford was smiling. It was bitterly cold and the wind slashed her face and hands like a razor as he laughed and held out a hand, and although she couldn't hang on to the mountainside she knew if she took his hand he would drag her into darkness.

When she woke she was huddled into the sleeping bag, her face buried. She could have been screaming but she hadn't been. It was deathly quiet. A scream would have stirred echoes, stirred the man who was sleeping, rolled in a blanket well away from her.

She sat up almost sobbing, but silently, as though breaking the silence would have started an avalanche. She had never known a silence like it. It was like being buried alive. There were shutters at the windows, so she could see nothing there, and suddenly she was terrified that more snow had fallen.

He had said there was more on the way, when there would be no path in or out of here. Perhaps the heavy falls had come a few weeks early and she was a prisoner here. Rafe would manage. He could live like the Resistance had lived, and she would be his prisoner.

She strained to hear, and now she thought there was a soft pattering, like snowflakes on a roof, and she could imagine the plateau and the ledge that had been frozen hard, waist deep in drifts by morning, white quicksands over which there could be no passing.

She had to see. She got out of the sleeping bag and crept towards the door. There was a heavy wooden bar, but that had not been pulled across. Of course it hadn't—there was nothing to keep out up here.

The door had stuck again; maybe snow was piled against it, freezing it shut. Caroline tugged at it, whimpering, and then it opened and she peered outside.

No more snow had fallen. But the wind had dropped. There was not a breath of wind, not a stirring anywhere, and didn't that mean something weird was going to happen to the weather, when the wind that blew constantly stopped blowing?

She stepped outside into a frozen silence, so out of this world that she could still have been in a nightmare. Then the silence shattered as Rafe roared her name. 'Caroline! What the hell are you doing?'

He was in the doorway and coming after her, and she thought, It is a nightmare; I'm going to be with him until I die.

Panic and anger rose in her like madness and she raised her hand and struck him across the face with a blow so violent and unexpected that he staggered back.

# CHAPTER FOUR

THE next thing Caroline knew, she was back in the house. She had either blacked out or been in such a blind panic that she was beyond registering anything.

Now she was huddled against the table's edge, staring down at her clenched fist, and she could not have been more horrified if her fingers had been clutching a knife. She moaned, 'I had a nightmare.'

'Were you sleepwalking?'

'No. Yes, in a way. I thought it had been snowing again. I thought we were never going to get down.'

Rafe said, 'I thought you'd gone looking for the Cave of the Winds.'

'You didn't!' That got through her trauma because it was so absurd.

'I suppose the door opening woke me. I sat up and looked and you weren't there, and that was the first thing that came into my head.'

She said dully, 'You must think I'm crazy.'

'A touch.' He smiled, and her lips quivered, but not with laughter, and her voice was unsteady as she said,

'I'd have been back inside in another three seconds flat. It's scary out there. The wind's dropped—it's unbelievable.'

'Not for long. It's just getting its breath.' That was the sort of thing you would say to a child, she thought, and she must be sounding childish.

She muttered, 'I shouldn't have pestered you to bring me up here. I've been a terrible muisance.'

'*You've* been unbelievable,' he said. 'You look like a piece of porcelain but you don't break.' He fingered his jaw. 'And you pack a mean punch.'

It wouldn't have surprised her if he had hit her back out there. That had been no token slap she'd given him—she had lashed at him with all her strength. She had never been violent in her life, and she looked at her hands again as if they were a stranger's. They were white with the cold and shaking uncontrollably, and so was she.

She was almost sobbing as she told him, 'I'm sorry, I lost my head; I've never hit anyone before and when I do I pick on somebody twice my size. Oh, lord. . . oh, I'm sorry. And now I'm getting hysterical. That's something else I've never done, but if I don't cry or scream or something I shall go out of my mind.'

Then she was sobbing, not tears but great, raucous gasps that hurt her chest, while her shoulders shook and her nervous system seemed to be unravelling. If Rafe hadn't held her up she would have fallen down. But soon, very soon, she was feeling better, a long way from strong but not far from gathering her wits together again. It had been like thrashing around in a whirlpool and finding something that held you steady and brought you ashore.

He held her until she stopped shaking, and then, sitting beside her on the table's edge, he began to rub her hands, and right away Caroline could feel sensation in them prickling hot and cold. His hands were gentle and strong, massaging her fingers, her palms, the backs of her hands.

It was a disturbingly sensual experience and she gave a little moan of pleasure, then tried to turn it into a laugh, a joke, saying, 'Your mother says you can always tell a lady by her hands.'

'The rubbish she talks,' he said. 'But your hands must have pleased her.'

This time her smile was spontaneous and real. 'I don't think she meant hands that pack a punch! But while I was clawing my way up here I thought that if I broke any nails I'd have to have false ones when I went back.'

He examined both hands. 'But you didn't.'

'They're very thick gloves.'

'Well, don't congratulate yourself too soon—we've got to get down yet.'

'Isn't it easier going down?'

'You can't be sure of anything on the mountains.'

'Don't I know it!' she said, and he smiled and loosed her hands and said,

'Get back in the sack; I'll get the fire going.'

This time she took off her boots and wriggled her toes down into the softness of the sleeping bag. It was incredible how that brief breakdown had washed the tension out of her. She was tired, of course, but not with the tortured exhaustion that had allowed her no real rest as though she was still fighting.

She sat with her knees hunched, her dark red hair falling loose on her shoulders, at peace for the first time since she had met Rafe Drayford again. It was no wonder that the climb up here had nearly finished her when she had been battling against the man as well as the mountain.

He was the reason Caroline had been so tense even before they had started. All the way her muscles had been strained like those of an animal at bay. And why? No harm could come from letting herself relax with him. He was a man she hardly knew at all, except from hearsay, and why shouldn't she form her own opinion?

He was not her enemy, although she had carried on as if he were. He was her ally, her comrade, which put a different slant on everything. Being stuck up here in this rugged shelter with a wilderness outside and another challenging day waiting for her tomorrow, was suddenly an exciting adventure and what she had come here looking for. It was better than she could have hoped, getting into the mountains with a guide she could trust with her life.

A rosy glow seemed to have settled around her. A pale rosy glow that was partly because there had been a fire in the hearth and some ashes still smouldered. She must have slept through that. She pulled the sleeping bag up to her chin and watched Rafe at the far end of the room, examining a chair.

'You're not thinking of pulling that apart?' she said, and he waved an axe at her.

'Are you as good at chopping as you are at slugging?'

'That was a one-off. You can't chop up the furniture.'

'It's hardly Chippendale. The owners are friends of mine, and I'll replace this.'

There was a lightness about her, as though a weight had been lifted from her shoulders. A glow and a light-heartedness that made her hug herself under the covers and smile at the sight of the man chopping up wood to keep her warm.

When the chair was logs he lit a lamp that burned as a wick in oil, which had been waiting for them here. Then he coaxed the embers and blew on the little flames and the wood caught at last, the dampness in it smoking and spluttering.

Even her weariness was pleasant. She rested her chin on her knees and asked, 'What else did we bring?' She had brought nothing, but they were partners.

The backpack was on the table. He touched the contents beside it, reeling them off. 'Lighter, torch, first-aid kit, flask of coffee, flask of soup, hip flask of brandy, chocolate, bedding.'

'We were well-equipped.'

He came and sat down beside here where she was huddled in her sleeping bag, telling her, 'I thought we'd only be away a few hours, but I thought you might need food and warmth at some stage.'

'I did. I do. I'm glad you packed an overnight bag. I just needed everything a bit higher up the mountain.'

There was nothing of the old elegant Rafe Drayford in this man. Although the face still had the high cheekbones, the long nose, the hard mouth, this was another man she had met when she had come to the village, with whom she had climbed a mountain and found a refuge.

A shadow of stubble was showing along his jawline. Some of the shadow might be a bruise, although his skin would not bruise easily. She would have liked to run her fingertips more or less where she had hit him and check for tenderness. Instead she bit her lip and said, 'You didn't expect to get slugged for your trouble.'

He seemed to have shrugged it off but she would never forget the frustration and panic that had been building up in her ever since she had seen him again, and that had climaxed in her first act of violence.

'Quite a lot about you I didn't expect,' he said.

He looked into her face as if she still puzzled him,

but with an intensity that was as intimate as if he had put a hand on her breast. 'Strange hair,' he said.

'What?'

'Hair so dark, and you so pale.'

'A mix-up, aren't I?' Her colouring had always been a dramatic contrast, and the way she felt now was nearer the dark fire of her hair than Christopher's lily-girl. She said, 'Now your hair suits you.'

It was wild and thick, springing back from his temples and forehead, curling over the collar of his shirt. She reached across to touch it and her fingers tingled so that she drew back, although she would have liked to run her hands deeper, holding his head and drawing his mouth closer to hers.

He lifted a lock of her hair, holding her gently by it and smiling down at her. 'It's as well we're in deep freeze up here,' he said, and she knew he was feeling, as she was, an incredible surge of physical awareness.

She nodded, agreeing that there was safety of a sort in being swaddled from neck to toes. 'Although,' he said, and smiled a crooked and wicked smile as she waited, 'if we rubbed together we would set the house on fire.'

That started her laughing. 'Only if we couldn't find two stones to rub together,' she said, 'and if you'd chopped up all the furniture. We're not going to get marooned up here, are we?'

'Very unlikely.' He reached for the slab of chocolate, and this time she took a piece; as it melted in her mouth she thought it tasted smoother and richer than any chocolate she had eaten before, as if even her taste buds were sharper.

'What would happen if we were?' With most of her

under the bedding, that was like saying, Tell me a story; and he humoured her, saying,

'Well, there's no shortage of water, and we could keep the fire going. Food might be a problem. There's a cheese hut near here, and we might find potatoes and that sort of thing in the houses. We might trap a wild goat or bring down a buzzard.'

She grimaced, and he laughed, 'Or I could get down and come back for you with a rescue team. Or we could winch you off by helicopter.'

She said with mock solemnity, 'I wouldn't care for being left behind while you went off. That wouldn't appeal to me at all. I think I'd have to go with you.'

'I thought you might.'

Suddenly she was no longer fooling. She said, 'Thank you for everything, I'll never forget any of it. I don't know why coming here mattered so much to me but it did.'

Her grandfather could have sheltered in this house his life almost over, although he was younger than Rafe Drayford was now. She said sadly, 'He was so young when he died and there were only a few more weeks to go. I don't know what happened.'

'A sniper on the road to Herakleion,' he said.

'Giorgio told you that?'

'Yes.'

Caroline's eyes filled with tears, and she turned her head into his shoulder as though his arm around her was her natural support. The leather of his jacket was clammy but the male vitality of the man warmed her, and now she was talking to him so easily. 'I don't think my grandmother knew that. She never talked about him; I don't think she remembered him well. She had the baby, my father, but she'd always gone on living in

the village shop with her parents, her life hardly
changed at all.

'When I go back there'll be nobody to tell. My father
wouldn't listen. He's a good man, my father; you
remember him?'

'Of course.'

Her parents remembered Rafe Drayford but she
hadn't told them about the letter his mother had asked
her to deliver. That would worry them to death, but
what she had learned about Danni in the White
Mountains wouldn't interest them.

She said, 'My father was Danni's son, but this doesn't
seem to have anything to do with him. Only with me.'

'You're a throwback.' He smiled down into her face
and he was almost right. There was a wildness in her.
In the mountains she was more her grandfather's child
than her father's.

Her hair was falling across her eyes so that she saw
his dark face through her own dark hair, and as he
brushed it back again his touch seemed to charge it
with electricity. She almost expected sparks to fly.

'How about you?' He was like none of his family she
knew, and she went on, 'Your family tree goes back
forever.' Dozens of Drayfords were buried in the local
churchyard. They had a vault to themselves and mem-
orial plaques around the walls of the church with the
usual flattering inscriptions. 'Not a lot of black sheep
there,' she teased.

'Not in living memory,' he agreed. 'My parents and
my parents' parents. . .model citizens every one. Well,
I don't have to tell you.'

'You do not.' She shouldn't be laughing but she was.

'We're mavericks, you and I,' he said. 'Two of
a kind.'

'Throwback and Maverick,' she gave it a sonorous ring, 'sounds like a firm of lawyers out of Dickens.'

'Would you put your lawsuit in our hands?' he quipped, and she capped that with,

'You want the best in dirty deals, we've got 'em.'

Then she remembered that he had been a lawyer. A good one, they said, although his lifestyle had not satisfied him and his break from it had been final. He would never return to the family firm and the family home.

This time next week she would be the one who was back in Virginia Grove, waiting to be married in the spring, when the blossom would be out and sunshine would stream through the long windows into the beautiful rooms that would be her home for the rest of her life.

Strangely, it was remembering Virginia Grove that was making her shiver. She knew it was warm in this rugged shelter on the frozen peaks, while Virginia Grove seemed bitterly cold and she was chilled at the thought of it.

Rafe got up and put another log on the fire, easing it into place with the toe of his boot. When he turned back she unzipped the bag and he got in beside her and put his arms around her, and almost at once she stopped shivering and snuggled against him like a small animal in its lair. Smiling, safe and comfortable, Caroline mumbled, 'I suppose this is bundling.'

'What?'

'In early Victorian days, or even before then, country-folk let couples who weren't married sleep together so long as they kept a bolster between them.'

He laughed at that. 'Fascinating. Where did you get that from?'

'I don't know. From a book or a history lesson, I suppose. Talking of ancient rights, I did wonder once if the Drayfords were into droit de seigneur.'

The right of the lord of the manor to claim the first night of any village bride. . . That was strictly medieval, but the brass-rubbing panel of a Hugo Drayforde in the church showed a man in armour with the crossed feet of a Crusader. And she could imagine Rafe Drayford's dark aquiline face under a Crusader's helmet.

'That wasn't one of the perks they mentioned to me,' he said. 'All I was offered was a job for life that bored me rigid.'

'And Isabel.'

'A nice girl. She'd have bored you.'

'Why do you say that?'

'You've so little in common.'

'You thought I was Isabel when you first saw me.'

'Not for long. Your hair's the wrong colour, and when you started going up the track on all fours, glaring like a polecat, you weren't much like Isabel then. Even before you slugged me.'

She had been lying curled into the crook of his arm, staring dozily into the fire if she was looking anywhere. Now she viewed him with her head raised and she could see there wasn't a bruise on his chin. 'Didn't Isabel ever slug you?' she asked.

'No way would Isabel have gone beyond a gentle push.'

She might have done after you walked out on her, thought Caroline. Push might have turned to shove then if she could have got her hands on you.

'Anyhow,' she said, 'the droit de seigneur offer's

past its sell-by date. Times have changed. Women aren't for scooping up any more.'

'I wouldn't say that.'

'*What* did you say.' They were talking nonsense, but this was too chauvinist to let pass without protest.

'It isn't only sheep they rustle up here—the occasional bride gets abducted.'

'I can't believe that.'

'Ask Kyria Maria, Giorgio's wife.'

The little bright-eyed woman with the wrinkled nut-brown face, who smiled a lot. 'Giorgio *kidnapped* her?' Caroline gasped.

'With a little help from his friends. She was from a village on the other side of the gorge. The families were feuding even during the occupation, and when the war ended and Giorgio abducted Maria that kept the feud going for another ten years.'

'Didn't she mind?' That was a silly question.

'Ask her.' said Rafe.

Caroline didn't speak the language well enough for that, and it was hardly the kind of thing you would be asking a dignified old lady who certainly seemed happy. 'Does it still happen?'

'Not as often as sheep thieving.' He could be having her on, especially when he went on, 'But don't worry. It's a purely Cretan custom, so you're safe.'

'I'm sure I am. Besides,' she added mischievously, 'I'm under your protection.'

'So you are. It wouldn't go down well in Virginia Grove if I had to tell them you'd gone off with a mountain man.'

If they could see me now, she thought, they would think I had. I couldn't look more at home, and I couldn't feel more confortable and contented. And you look as if you've lived in the mountains all your life.

She asked, 'Where have you been for the past five years?'

'On the move.'

'Tell me.'

'So that you can report back?' His drawl was amused, and that *was* why she had searched for him, to deliver Anna Drayford's letter and to take back news of her elder son.

But now she said, 'No,' and wondered if she would tell them anything, except that he was fit and well. She said, 'I haven't been on the move. I've had holidays, of course, but this is my wildest trip. I envy you. Tell me where you've been and I'll close my eyes and pretend I was there.'

'With me?'

'Why not?'

'I can name a few reasons why not.'

He didn't have to name them—she knew he was too tough for her. He travelled fast, and light on baggage. She couldn't have kept up with him for five weeks, let alone nearly five years. He was smiling, and this was a game they were playing.

'Don't be so macho,' she teased. 'I was never far behind you on the mountain.'

'That's true.'

'The rope might have helped, but when you looked round I was there, wasn't I?'

'You were.'

'So, tell me, when did you first come to the village?'

In summer, he said, a couple of years after he walked out of an English village, he had sat on a hillside talking to a man more or less his own age. A Cretan

shepherd who, with the legendary hospitality of the
mountain folk, had taken him home for a meal. That
was the house he was using now. He had come back
there over the years, stayed with the family, and stayed
on this year when they had gone down to winter
quarters on the lowlands.

He told her the names of the wife, the children; and
she thought they seemed more his family than Robert
and Anna Drayford. And Yanni the shepherd was
closer to a brother than Christopher had been.

She said, hesitantly, 'If they wanted to see you, your
folk, you mother, this is where they could find you for
the winter months?' and he chuckled.

'Leaving my father out of this, can you see my
mother bouncing up the track to the village in a Jeep,
much less sitting down at the table for a meal? And if
she had to stay the night, do you think she'd prefer
being on the ledge or up the ladder.'

Caroline smiled, but her smile was wistful. 'It
wouldn't do, would it? I'll tell her you're all right.'

'Do that,' he said. 'I'll write to her from wherever I
am in the next few weeks.'

'Not here?'

He shrugged. 'Probably not.'

She wished he had been staying here. She would
have liked to know where he was, as if some time she
might need to get in touch, and not knowing where to
find him would be a calamity.

She asked, still hesitating, 'Would you—write to
me?' and he looked at her with a raised eyebrow so
that she said quickly, 'No, of course you couldn't. So,
where might you be going. . .where else have you
been?'

He told her more than anyone back home knew. His

letters home had always been brief, but for Caroline he filled in details, although she was sure this was a censored version and she was only getting the half of it.

He had travelled. He had hitched, worked, probably conned his way around the world, and he spun her a fascinating and funny saga so that it sounded great. But it couldn't all have been that good. Rafe Drayford was a man who would walk on the dark side as often as in the sunshine, seeking below the surface and coming up with lord knew what.

But he made her smile, describing some of the places and people, and what had happened to him among them, so vividly that she could imagine being there herself. And relaxing like this was as soothing as sleeping.

It was so restful, lying together, and this must have been what she had wanted all along. To be close to him, because they were two of a kind, and this little bed in a mountain hideout could have been a little boat they were drifting in.

All of it was dreamlike and natural and safe, and when he finished telling her about a fiesta in Peru she murmured, 'That must have been a happy day.'

'It was.' He shifted his position slightly, his arm still under her head, but leaning sidewards to look at her. 'Now it's your turn.'

'What is?' She found herself yawning as she spoke.

'Share a happy day. How's that for a slogan? Tell me about your good times.'

She had had lots of good times in a happy life. Happy but uneventful. But of course it hadn't been an uneventful life when she had fallen in love with Christopher and he with her.

'Somewhere well away from Virginia Grove, if you could manage that,' said Rafe.

'All right. Although my highspots will probably bore you.'

'What I don't need,' he said, 'is anything to get me excited,' and she giggled like a schoolgirl, and felt a tingle of excitement running down her spine.

'Something calming,' she said. 'Let me think.' After a moment she asked, 'Do you swim?'

'Yes.'

'One night I swam out to a rock. I was on holiday with my parents in Cornwall, and the hotel overlooked a bay and there was this rock right out to sea. I'd swum there in the daytime. It was a good summer; you may have forgotten but we do still get them. During the day there were always swimmers around, this was late when they'd all gone to bed, and the moon was out and the sea was dark, and I swam out there and lay on the rock.'

It had been earlier this year, when she had just got engaged to Christopher. She had swum out because she enjoyed swimming, and having the sea all to herself had seemed irresistible when she had woken up and gone on to her bedroom balcony and looked out on it.

Being alone on the rock had been part of her pleasure, but now, as she described how it was, she could imagine a dark swimmer keeping pace beside her, a man hauling himself out of the sea and her with him, water streaming from their gleaming bodies. She wondered if his hair sleeked down when it was wet, and said, 'I've never told anybody about that—it would have scared my mother so. Welcome to my rock.'

'I'll cherish that,' he said.

'I walk miles over the moors at home,' she said.

'And the Yorkshire Dales—I've had some happy times walking over the Dales.'

That had been on holidays again, and often she had walked alone. Now as she talked she took Rafe Drayford with her, his image imprinting so powerfully on the pictures in her mind that she might never again be certain that he had not been physically with her.

She knew she was not invading his memories like this, and she said, 'Think about me if you ever go back to Acapulco.'

'I will.' He touched her cheek and she flinched. 'A scratch,' he said, but she hadn't felt that, only his touch, and she remembered.

'I got it last night on your pillow.'

'I did warn you it was rough.' He smiled the crooked smile she was beginning to know so well. 'Not a mark on you from the mountain,' he said. 'You get your scars before you start.'

'It won't scar. It's nothing, and I heal quickly.' She had healed from little cuts and grazes. She had never had a wound deep enough to leave a lasting scar.

Rafe kissed her cheek, not her mouth, but the rush of sensation was overwhelming. She put up a shaking hand and the rubies in her ring seemed darker than ever against her skin, and the ring seemed heavier. She had forgotten the ring, and she stared at it now.

'Shall we roll up the bolster?' he said, and his face swam mistily above her, and she could feel him against her skin, through their layered clothing, as though she lay naked in his arms.

If she even slipped off her jacket there was a very real danger that she would go up in flames, and she took a steadying breath before she managed to say, 'I'd rather not,' as if she was saying no to more coffee.

'Good thinking.' Caroline felt he had only been half serious. A kiss on the cheek was nothing unless the next kiss went deeper. It had shaken her and it had stirred him, but his conscience wouldn't be troubling him. He would have had no scruples about temporarily stealing his brother's woman. But if she cheated with Rafe she could never face Christopher again, and she loved Christopher. This was mountain madness and she was thankful that Rafe was accepting her 'good thinking' with good humour.

He still held her. There was room for the two of them so long as they huddled together. She was doing most of the curling up. His arm was around her, enfolding her, and in spite of her bulky clothing she felt quite tiny.

His voice was deeper than Christopher's, slower. 'We can't go on swapping life stories all night,' he said, 'and you won't let me make love to you, so perhaps we should go to sleep. We've got to climb down in the morning.'

She was still a novice, a rank beginner as a climber. The track had been a deadly obstacle course and would be again. She should be sleeping, but she wasn't sure she wanted to because she was so comfortable, drowsing like this. And she wanted to go on talking.

There were still things she wanted to ask him. She would have liked to know more about Elpida. And the other women. He had spoken of women, and men, but not of affairs.

There must have been affairs. There had been a smouldering sensuality about him in the old days, but mentally and physically he had developed into a most disturbingly sexy man. She murmured, 'I don't think I'll sleep.' and he said,

'Yes, you will,' and there was something so soothing in the way he was holding her. She was not being rocked but she felt as if she were. Moving with his breathing, and her own, she felt cherished and comforted, and surprisingly soon she was sleeping soundly.

Caroline woke to a moment of having no idea where she was; then her darting eyes took in the rough boards of the ceiling and the stone walls and she raised her head to see Rafe at the door. Oh, good! she thought.

He opened the door and from here she could see the whiteness like a curtain, beginning to wisp like smoke. Oh, God! she thought. She croaked, 'Snow?'

'Mist.'

'Is that as bad as snow?'

'It disperses quicker.'

She tried to sit up and every muscle in her seemed locked: arms, shoulders, back, legs. Her entire body was starting to ache and she gave a howl of pain. As he came towards her she moaned, 'I'm paralysed.' His lips twitched and she snarled, 'Don't you dare laugh.'

'I wouldn't think of it. I hadn't thought of this either.'

She hadn't expected this degree of stiffness. She was fit—she swam, played tennis, did workouts—but climbing the mountain must have used different muscles, and she had been so tense all the time, which put a double strain on her body. Now she had morning-after stiffness and, although it was neither dangerous nor chronic, it *hurt*.

'I was all right when I woke before,' she wailed. But since then she had lain hardly moving, and now it was agony to move.

'We should have made love,' he said, and of course

he was laughing. 'Sex might have reached the parts that were seizing up.'

She said huffily, 'Don't be ridiculous, and start thinking about how I'm getting down. And don't you say you'll winch me off by helicopter.'

'I could carry you.'

'So you said earlier. Swung over your shoulder, I seem to remember you saying.' She was in a foul temper. Caroline Hammond of the sweet nature was spitting mad because she was helpless and good for a laugh. 'How long will the mist last?' she demanded as if he were to blame for its arrival.

'The wind's rising again. That shifts it.'

'Hours? Days?' As she said 'days' her breath caught.

'Hours,' he said. 'It's probably clear further down, but we could miss the track in visibility this bad.'

He began to make up the fire and she started to wriggle, very slowly and carefully, under the covers. She had to get moving although all she wanted to do was lie still, and she was realising for the first time how hard the ground was under the sleeping bag.

Last night it had seemed quite soft. She had been so tired and she had slept slumped against Rafe Drayford. This morning, though, she was keeping some space between him and her. There was altogether too much animal magnetism about him and right now she was aching with muscle fatigue, not lust. She had enough on her mind wondering how she was going to stumble down to the village without letting herself start fancying Christopher's brother again.

Rafe was taking no notice of her now, concentrating on the fire, and he had it burning brightly, the wood crackling, before she felt up to standing up. She crawled out of the sleeping bag, grabbing the table for support and painfully pulling herself nearly upright.

He turned to watch her, and because he looked concerned she grinned wryly. 'I feel like the tin man in *The Wizard of Oz*, who got rusted up. I ought to be creaking.'

'Is it bad?'

'It's bad, but I think it's just stiffness. I've never had it like this before—I can stand, but it's moving that worries me.' She took a few steps and winced, groaning, 'Oh, for a hot bath!'

'They oiled the tin man,' he said and put an earthenware jar on the table. She sniffed and wrinkled her nose. 'Top grade olive oil,' he said, which he knew ought to bring back some of her suppleness.

Slowly she got out of her trousers and pulled off the long stockings. He laid the blanket in front of the fire for her and she went cautiously down on it, the oil pot beside her.

Darkish oil dripped from her fingers as she began to rub it into the calves of her legs. All her muscles felt sore. Her shoulders ached as she bent over her task, and she gave an involuntary whimper.

'Here, let me.' Rafe had taken off his jacket and rolled up his sleeves; she couldn't have stiffened more but she sat rigid, on the defensive.

'No, thanks, I can manage.'

'Pretend it's suntan oil,' he said, and if someone she knew and quite liked offered to rub protective cream on her on a beach she wouldn't be as prudish. She still hesitated, but when he poured oil into the palms of his hands, rubbed them together and began to massage the knotted muscles of her knees, she gave a weary sigh then lay back and closed her eyes.

The fire threw out enough heat to be summer sunshine. She could hear the wind and imagine it was the sighing of the sea. She could have been lying on a rock. . .this was too hard for sand, but they could both have swum out to her rock in the Cornish bay. . .and the practised touch of healing hands was working magic.

He was good. Artists' hands were strong and sensitive, but she must not let herself get aroused. She would pretend there were other swimmers circling them, and let the sunshine and the oil sink deep into her skin, warming her blood and easing her aches.

'Do a lot of this, do you?' she asked. She didn't mean stroking a woman in a way that went beyond the surface. She was not flirting, and neither, it seemed, was he.

'First time I've been landed with a girl who got muscle-bound on a mountain top,' he said.

'We're not at the top.'

'True.' She could bend her knee now, both of her knees, but when he asked, 'Do you feel like going for the Cave of the Winds?' she yelped before she saw that he was grinning. Then she said emphatically,

'*Never*. If I'd climbed any further I could have spent the rest of the winter up here like a hermit, and only managed to hobble down in the spring. But I think I've got the use of my legs back. That oil's powerful stuff.'

'I told you. The best. Now we'll do your shoulders.'

She was no more embarrassed than she would have been peeling off outer clothing on a beach. She got back into stockings and trousers, and took off her sweater and thermal top, and lay face down while he worked the oil into her shoulder blades and down her spine.

She was feeling easier all the time and as her arms and elbows were getting the treatment she murmured, 'Much more oil and I'll be able to slide down the mountain.'

'Are we overdoing it?'

'Don't you know?'

'No, actually. I just presumed you poured it on and worked it in.'

She sat up. 'You're a quack—I thought you knew how to massage!'

'It's working, isn't it? You couldn't have done any better. You couldn't even move.'

She couldn't deny that she was in much better shape than she'd been half an hour ago. She was covered in oil, but her joints were in working order. She sniffed an arm. 'I smell like a sardine, the tinned variety.'

'Nothing wrong with sardines.'

She began to get into the rest of her clothes. He might not know the regulation moves but he certainly had the touch. She was glowing and hungry. She said, 'I could murder a tin of sardines right now.'

'I'll take mine fried over charcoal with half a lemon.'

'Toast would be nice. Buttered toast and marmalade.'

'Half a cup of lukewarm soup or a piece of chocolate?' That was what they had, and she said,

'Chocolate, please,' and sucked on a square while she laced up her boots.

They wouldn't go hungry. Rafe would cope. He would either get them down the mountain or find food somehow from somewhere. Considering the grimness of their situation, Caroline was beginning to feel remarkably cheerful, ready and eager to get on with the day.

When he opened the door she stood beside him looking out, seeing that the mist was no longer solid out there. There were breaks in it now, a thinning, and he said, 'Stay here; I'll check beyond the ledge.'

'I'll come.' He put her aside literally, with light but firm hands on her shoulders, as she protested, 'I'd much rather stay with you.'

'No. I won't be long.'

He closed the door and he had gone, and of course she would have been a hindrance he could do without, but almost at once her isolation hit her. While he was near she had been so sure that everything would be all right. Alone she was as vulnerable as a toddling child.

Suppose he did not come back? Even a little fall could break a leg or hit a head against a rock. Two might have been safer than one, she thought; she should have gone with him, he should have let her go.

Time passed, dragging, and she stood in the open doorway and called his name. Only once, because the wind turned her cry into a banshee howl, and she wasn't calling that up again. The mist was making swirling white shapes across the little plateau and between the houses, like dancing ghosts, but she stepped outside because it was no lonelier out here than it was in the empty house.

She crept around, striving to hear above the wind, straining her eyes for a solid shape coming through the mist, and when she saw him the relief nearly knocked her off her feet.

She saw him below her as she came round a house, and she leaned against the wall as he shouted at her as he had done the last time, 'What the *hell* are you doing?'

'I came to meet you.' She was elated with relief,

chattering gaily, 'You were away a long time and the mist's clearing.'

'Stay where you are.' He came up level with her, and in seconds was beside her, gripping her arm. 'Look down,' he said.

She looked down and out, and quite soon the ledge fell away quite steeply. She had been watching where she was going, and she wouldn't have fallen off, but he obviously thought she might have done. She said again, 'You were away a long time.'

'I was away less than ten minutes.'

'It seemed longer.' Much longer. She tried to lighten the moment. 'There's dancing in the square—the mist's making dancing ghosts,' but she got no answering smile.

His voice was grim. 'If you'd gone off this ledge you could have been dancing with ghosts. We can get down now, and don't make a move unless I'm watching you.'

He held her arm for the short distance back to the house, but somehow she knew he was losing patience with her and the time of laughter was over.

# CHAPTER FIVE

INSIDE the house Rafe began packing the backpack. Caroline watched him folding bedding into small neat squares, slotting in flasks and containers, and marvelled how quietly and deftly all was being cleared away.

She wondered stupidly if she should be leaving a note saying, 'Thank you for the shelter; I had a lovely time, and I shall certainly recommend your bed-and-breakfast to my friends.'

That was a joke not worth repeating, especially as he seemed no longer in a jokey mood. He was amiable enough, however, and he talked to her as he packed, telling her that the mist was mostly on the higher slopes and they should get down without too much difficulty, slowly, of course, but they ought to be moving in case it came down again. And, as snow was always a possibility, the sooner they started out the better.

She listened and nodded and said, 'Yes,' and, 'Of course,' and thought how capable he sounded. That was good. That was what she needed. But the intimacy had gone, so that it was hard to believe they had nearly made love last night. So very nearly that the memory of it lingered in the core of her being as though he had reached deep inside her.

Only it was not a memory because it had not happened, and this morning she was very glad that it had not. If it had she would have been racked with guilt by now.

He was in a hurry to get away. Weather conditions

made that common sense, and she watched him buck-
ling up the backpack and damping down the fire with
snow, although there was surely no danger of sparks
igniting anything in here.

He had the backpack strapped to his shoulders now.
Caroline zipped up, with hat on and hood up, booted
and gloved. And roped. She wasn't arguing about the
rope, as she could easily be slithering off the path.

'Ready?' he said and smiled, and she smiled back
and thought, Even his smile is different. There is no
closeness between us. If I moved too near he would
raise an eyebrow and set me aside, as he did just before
he went out alone into the mist.

Last night was over and done with, and one of the
reasons he was wasting no time getting her back to
where her car was waiting could be because he wanted
to be rid of her, and she babbled, 'Will we be down
before dark?'

'I can guarantee it.'

They came out of the house, closing the door,
crossing the little plateau through the trailing mist, with
the wind screaming around them. She had to raise her
voice to be heard as she said 'It's been incredible—
thank you again. But what I want now is a hotel with a
bathroom. I'm so oily I'll need to soak for hours.'

'Don't worry,' he said. 'You'll be back in civilisation
soon.' He wasn't suggesting she stay any longer, and
she had done everything she came out here to do—met
the old freedom fighters, gone into the mountains.

They were not two of a kind, Caroline and Rafe
Drayford. They were poles apart in almost every way.
They were roped together now, with he guiding her
every step, but once down the mountain she would be
on the road to civilisation and home.

Nobody knew where he would be, until another letter arrived at Virginia Grove with maybe another address. His mother would hardly be sending Caroline after him twice, so when she left the village she would probably never see him again and it wouldn't worry her. Two days and two nights in his company had been quite enough.

It was not easier climbing down. Sometimes it was harder, because when you were looking down the risk of slipping seemed greater. When stones shifted beneath her feet she went rigid, some of the stiffness coming back into her bones.

They rested briefly a couple of times, out of the wind under overhanging rock, and she was tiring. But she was not fighting the man this time. On this trip he was a supportive guide, setting a pace she could manage, helping her over the worst patches.

Mist lingered patchily for hours, but he kept them on the winding path down even when she could see no trace of a track although most of the time she could make out the village below. She was longing to reach it. Not with the frantic urge she had felt to reach the snowbound hamlet, but because warmth and food and shelter and her get-away car were waiting for her there.

They passed the shepherd's hut, coming into the summer grazing lands, and they were within hailing distance of the village when she slipped. Her concentration had wandered for a moment; she had heard the tinkling of a goat-bell and looked around for the animal, stepping on a patch of ice under the snow and whooshing down on her bottom.

Again she did not fall far, this time the rope checking her, and almost before Rafe was picking her up she was scrambling to her feet. 'Let's try not to arrive on our backs,' he said, and she nearly swore at him, although he hadn't pushed her. It was not his fault she had slipped but he could still irritate her with his snide superiority.

Funny that, she thought, brushing the snow off the seat of her trousers, I feel the same about him now as I did before we set off. Up there I went a little snow crazy, fancying him like mad; down here, nearly in the village again, I think that Christopher's brother is everything that Christopher said he was.

She gritted her teeth and kept her mind on her slow progress, every step bringing her closer to the village and nearer cutting loose from Rafe Drayford. She unroped herself as they came down behind the house, into the lane leading to the church and the square.

A man called across from one of the houses and Rafe answered. Rafe was saying they'd reached the hamlet, because the man glanced up at it and then nodded and smiled, and Caroline thought, It doesn't surprise him. He thinks that Danni's granddaughter would manage to get up there.

It had been a near thing. The way she felt now, the climb had half killed her, but she found herself smiling back, straightening up and stepping out almost jauntily on her wobbly legs.

There were more greetings and more exchanges before they reached the house where Rafe was staying, and where Elpida was waiting for them. She was sitting by the hearth and she jumped up and came hurrying over when he opened the door. She was smiling and very beautiful, her dark hair with its heavy waist-length plait shining like silk, and she was still wearing the golden earrings.

She went to Rafe and he put an arm around her,

pulling her towards him. Leaning against him, she turned her head just enough to direct a slanting triumphant smile at Caroline, and Caroline wondered if she should be taking off her glove and flashing her ring to emphasise which brother it was in whom she had a vested interest.

There was a murmur of Greek between them. Not sweet nothings, just words, as he slipped off the backpack and Caroline moved nearer the warmth of the stove. Considering how little she knew of the language, she bet she could follow what they were saying: he said they had reached the hamlet, and Elpida said, fancy that, and when was Caroline leaving? Not today, he said, which disappointed Elpida, and Caroline was so sure she was getting the drift of it that she said, 'Tomorrow, early,' and when he raised an eyebrow and translated she knew that she was right.

'I thought you couldn't speak the language,' he said.

'I can read body language.' She sat down just before her knees gave way. 'And while we're on the subject of bodies, is there any chance of some hot water? I'm soaked in oil.'

The buzz of having lived up to her grandfather's reputation by climbing so high was suddenly draining away. Elpida's exuberance was the last thing she needed right now. Of course, it had nothing to do with the way Elpida had run to Rafe and he had put an arm around her. Their intimacy was not depressing Caroline—being bone weary was.

There was a black iron kettle on the stove with steam coming from the spout, and he lifted it, checking its fullness. 'Hot water's limited to this unless you wait while we boil up more.'

'Can I have that for now?'

'Surely.' He carried a tin bowl to a place nearer the stove and told her, 'I'll be in the house next door on the left when you're through. You have soap, a towel?'

'Both.' He'd seen them, examining her luggage before they had set out.

'Sorry there's not enough to soak in,' he said, 'But it will make the bathroom you get tomorrow seem palatial.'

'Tomorrow can't come soon enough.' That was blurted out, and it was ungrateful after the trouble she'd been and the way she was imposing now. She tried to moderate her tactlessness, adding, 'Just for the bathroom,' and he smiled his crooked smile.

'I know exactly what you mean.'

He poured boiling water into the bowl; and Elpida banged down a jug of cold water beside it, wearily, as if this was carrying hospitality too far. 'Thank you,' said Caroline.

As they went through the front door into the street she heard Elpida laughing, and wondered if she would be quite so merry if she had known that most of the oil covering most of Caroline had been applied by Rafe Drayford's hands.

She shot the wooden bolts on both doors, although even with the heat from the stove she was not sure she could endure stripping off. There was only enough hot water to sponge herself down, and if she didn't hurry that would have cooled and she wouldn't need to add any cold.

She scrambled up the ladder to fetch her bags, and in front of the stove she pulled out towel and soap, face flannel, face tonic and body lotion. Then she peeled off to her waist and went down on her knees in front of the bowl, rubbing fast and hard with the

soaped flannel, mopping off, and shifting more of the
oil with tonic on a rolled-up pair of tights.

She got into a clean bra and vest and out of the rest
of her climbing gear, washing herself from the waist
down with the same frantic speed.

Finally she dressed herself in the clothes she had
worn when she had come to the village, and wondered
whether to dump the rest. Her inner clothing was
saturated and the linings of her outer wear had a
clinging smell of oil. But she had been madly extrava-
gant when she had bought all this and so she packed
the outer wear into her case. It could always be cleaned
some time, and, although she wouldn't be mountain
climbing again, she could always give it away to a
friend or a charity.

She had arrived here wearing jeans and a polo
necked Aran sweater, under a padded jacket and a
long red scarf. In jeans and sweater she was almost
back to normal, except for the twinges still lurking in
some of her muscles, although she could hardly believe
that she looked the same.

There was oil in her hair too but she brushed it into
loose deep waves, and then she creamed her face and
touched her lips and her cheekbones with a coral
colour. She hesitated for a moment, holding the mascara wand, then shrugged and did her usual discreet
eye make-up, which brought out gold flecks in her
hazel eyes.

The last three days had been fantastic but she was
glad they were over. She might tell Mrs Drayford that
Rafe had taken her sightseeing into the mountains. Not
that they had spent a night up there. Christopher would
not understand that.

She could tell his mother Rafe was painting. That

sounded interesting and nearly respectable. She wondered if she should ask if she might take a picture back with her, although those vibrant colours would be out of place in Virginia Grove, where everything seemed to be muted and dim.

She was getting some odd ideas while she was here and the sooner she left the better. She should be packing now. It wouldn't take long but she wanted everything ready for leaving early.

She was packing upstairs when somebody rapped on the street door and brought her hurrying down again. Rafe was alone out there, asking, as he came into the house, 'Are you all right?'

'Yes. Why shouldn't I be?'

'You were taking your time, considering you'd only got a kettleful of water. I wondered if you'd fallen asleep.'

She was not too clear in her mind or steady on her feet but she managed a grin. 'You'd be surprised how far a little hot water goes if you soap yourself fast.'

'I can imagine,' he said, and that brought colour into her face that she tried to hide by fiddling with her hair. 'You look perfect,' he said, 'flawless,' but the compliment was ironic.

She said, 'The perfection's only skin deep. I got it out of my make-up bag. I've nearly finished packing. Are you sure you don't want to write a letter for me to take back?'

'Tell her I'll be in touch.'

'Any messages for the rest of your family?'

'Say hello to my father for me, and congratulate Christopher. On finding the right girl.'

For a split-second she hadn't known why Christopher was being congratulated, although it was an obvious message for Rafe to send to his brother, and he was probably sincere because he had said from the beginning how suitable she was for Christopher Drayford and all that went with him.

But now she was too weary to care. She sat down in one of the rush-seated chairs and put her folded arms on the table, her head resting on her arms muffling her voice as she said, 'If I go to sleep now and sleep all night I might be awake for tomorrow.'

'You should eat first. They have a meal waiting for us next door,' and she raised her head and groaned,

'I couldn't live through another party.'

He was smiling at her but he wasn't touching her. 'Just a meal. You get to bed and I'll fetch you some food.'

She thought woozily, You're always telling me to go to bed. 'Get into that,' you said when you unrolled the bedroll, and, 'Get back in the sack,' after I nearly knocked you out and then started sobbing on your shoulder.

She said 'That would be a lovely idea.'

It might not be another rave-up next door but there would be a lot of folk, and Elpida would be there, clutching Rafe's arm and showing Caroline that she might be Danni's granddaughter but she was still an outsider and this was goodbye.

Tomorrow morning she would wave goodbye, smiling and thanking them all, but she could not face them now. She stood up and said brightly, 'If you ever come to my house I'll see you get breakfast in bed.'

What was she talking about? Not Virginia Grove. That would be her house, her home, but he would never come there. 'One good turn deserves another,' she said. 'And I'll tell you something else—I might never climb another mountain but I'm getting the knack of hopping up and down that ladder.'

He shook his head at her, smiling, as if she was talking nonsense, and so she was. She went up the ladder and sat on the floor to take off her shoes, feeling so miserable that she was near to tears.

She hoped Elpida would not come up with the supper.

Caroline was not a welcome guest to Elpida, but a link with another life for Rafe. Although Caroline reckoned that Elpida would dislike and distrust any young woman who had the slightest claim on Rafe Drayford.

Not that Caroline had a claim. She had brought a letter and told him why she was here, and he had taken her to meet Giorgio and offered to be her guide into the mountains. He would probably have done the same for a stranger. But now he was through, and tomorrow she would say goodbye to him and Elpida would be there, smiling her smug little smile, so what had she got to be hostile about? She had the man, for God's sake!

Not, of course, that Caroline wanted him. Caroline had Christopher, and as soon as she was away from here she would start thinking about Christopher again. How handsome and super he was and how much she wanted to spend the rest of her life with him.

But here there had been a jolting of her spirit, throwing everything out of sync, and she lay on the canvas camp-bed under the heavy blanket, her thick hair keeping the roughness of the pillow from her skin, and started thinking again about the man she was going to marry.

The next holiday she took should be their honey-

moon, as soon as they had decided where to go out of
all the exciting options open to them. Anywhere but
the White Mountains. Christopher hadn't wanted her
to come here and she would never come back so long
as Rafe was here.

The trapdoor was open, so she heard the footsteps
on the hard earthen floor below and knew that it was
Rafe. She sat up and waited and even before he came
up, like a demon king in a pantomime, the image of
Christopher was shattered.

So long as she was in this village, with Rafe Drayford
looming over her, everything else seemed unreal.
Tomorrow would be different, and by the time she was
home again Rafe Drayford would be a fading memory.

He put a wooden tray down by the bed, and her bag,
which they had left next door for safe keeping, beside
it. 'All right?' he asked with a searching glance, and
she nodded.

'Uh-huh; dead beat but all right.'

'Eat and sleep,' he said.

There was more than enough for two but he was
leaving her, lowering the trapdoor after him, and she
called, 'Have fun.'

'What makes you think you're the only one who's
dead beat?'

'Not you.' Not with Elpida hovering around, willing
and waiting.

'You expect some staying power from your men,
don't you?' He looked at her with mock horror. 'You
could be the death of Christopher.' He grinned at her
and she was laughing.

Neither of them had had much sleep last night and it
couldn't have been easy for him, getting up the mountain and down again. Elpida might not have such an

exciting night ahead after all, and suddenly Caroline couldn't stop smiling.

She *was* hungry. She buttered a hunk of bread and bit into it and thought how good food tasted here. Tomorrow it would be served more elegantly, and she wouldn't be using a knife like this to spread butter and hack cheese and spear the small sweet tomatoes. But she was hungry now.

She drank almost a tumbler of wine but it didn't matter. All she had to do was sleep, and tomorrow she would really spoil herself, booking into a good hotel. Then she would plan how she would spend the rest of her holiday in Crete.

She would go to Knossós, of course. This time of year there should be no crowds. She should be able to wander almost alone through the ruins of what had once been a palace of a thousand rooms. She wanted to see the Snake Goddess and the athletes vaulting along the backs of charging bulls—all manner of marvellous things.

And then she would go shopping for gifts to take home. It would be hard to find anything for Christopher. He must have everything he could possibly want, and the only thing Anna Drayford was waiting for was news of Rafe.

Caroline poured herself some more wine, gulping it down because she wanted it to send her to sleep so that tomorrow would come and she could get away.

She slept fitfully at first, and when she slept soundly at last, waking in daylight, she had the headache of a slight hangover.

She dug into her first-aid kit for painkillers and swallowed a couple, one sticking in her throat until she coughed it down. She gave herself a few more minutes' lying still before she got off the bed and into her shoes. Apart from shoes she had been fully dressed.

When she looked at herself in her little make-up mirror she wished she had not bothered with eye make-up yesterday. It was smudged now, and she tissued off most of the mascara. Then she combed her hair gently and managed to open the trapdoor without trapping her fingers.

Rafe was sitting at the table below. He looked up at her with a cheery, 'Good morning,' that she echoed on a more subdued note, enquiring,

'Would that be coffee you're drinking?'

'Yes. Are you ready for a cup?'

'More than ready.' She turned to pick up the tray and he said,

'Come down; I'll see to that.'

She might have coped with the balancing act or she might have let the dishes slide and crash. She decided not to chance it. She came down the ladder and left the tray to him, taking a mug from the table and pouring coffee from a pot on the stove. Then she sat down and breathed in the aroma of coffee as though it was a rare perfume.

'Are you all right?' The times he'd asked her that! More often than she had ever been asked in her life before. This time there was nothing really wrong with her and she pulled a face.

'It's my fault, but I've got a thick head from too much wine.' He had put the tray down on the table. He could see that the jug was nearly empty. It was always hard to tell what he was thinking, but now she guessed he was wondering if this was going to delay her departure, and she said, 'Not a bad one. I've taken aspirins and the coffee will fix it, so I'm all ready to go unless you've got an instant hangover cure.'

'They swear by pastas round here, and tripe soup.' He was smiling now, reassured that she wasn't hanging around, and her horror was only slightly exaggerated as she said,

'Don't even think of it—I'm much too fragile for tripe soup this time in the morning.'

'The rugged life's losing its appeal?'

'Well, it is time I moved on, did a little more sightseeing, a little shopping.'

'Like a proper tourist?'

'I am a proper tourist. I'm on holiday.'

'Of course you are,' he said. 'More coffee?'

By the time she had completed a quick toilet, washing hands and face in cold water at the sink, he had brought down her cases and neighbours were coming in to say goodbye, escorting her to her car and giving her a celebrity send-off.

When she climbed into the Jeep under the cypress tree she wound down the window. Rafe had opened the door and put in the cases. She was holding his hand through the window, smiling at him, smiling at everybody

'*Kali stratia*,' one old woman called, and he translated, 'She's wishing you a good road, a safe journey.'

'*Efharistó para polí*, thank you very much,' said Caroline, and he said,

'Very good.' His hand was still in hers. Then he said, 'Go home now and let Christopher take care of you,' and his fingers were no longer around hers, but Elpida still had hold of him.

They moved back as Caroline switched on the ignition and she drove the car towards the rocky road that led down from the village. When she turned for a final goodbye there was a flurry of waving hands, and all the faces were friendly. Rafe was not smiling but he raised a hand, and then she was sure he breathed a sigh of relief that she was no longer any responsibility of his.

She had to stop herself pressing her foot on the accelerator, which would have been madness on this road, as her headache began to pound again in sudden panic. She had believed she was anxious to get away but she had just realised that if Rafe had said 'Stay' she would have been out of the car with no hesitation.

She had to go but she wanted to stay, although staying would have been insane. Rafe Drayford was not just dangerous, he could be deadly, and while she was near him she was at risk of losing her head and plenty more besides. She had to get away, and because this whole island hadn't space enough to keep her safe she was leaving Crete as quickly as possible.

She bounced and bumped her car down the break-neck track, taking the broader and better road to Herakleion. Somewhere along this road, long ago, Danni had died from a sniper's bullet. Death had been commonplace in those days, but she grieved for the loss of his young life. And maybe some of her sadness was for herself, as if her own youth were ending.

Caroline was in Rhodes by the end of the day. She had caught the ferry from Crete, taken a taxi near the harbour, and given the name of a hotel where friends had stayed in the summer, coming back with glowing reports. She remembered the name, and a little way out of Rhodes town she arrived at an imposing hotel set against a pine-covered hillside.

Off season there was no problem booking in. She had moved from the rough and rugged to the seriously rich, and as soon as she was alone in her bedroom she took off her shoes, jeans and tights, and padded around barefoot on the jewel-coloured rugs, just for the pleasurable sensation of velvety pile tickling her toes.

Then she unpacked. She had left her oil-soaked undies behind, and what she had was mostly heavy winter wear. But she could buy anything more she might need. There were boutiques in the foyer, shops in the town. She had hardly touched her traveller's cheques and she could use credit cards.

But before anything else she must wash her hair and take that hot bath to get rid of the last traces of stickiness and stiffness. Undressing in the bathroom was a joy. Everything was warm and shining.

Caroline got under the shower first, lathering and conditioning her hair, shaking her tresses under the flowing water until every hair had to be squeaky clean. Then she ran the bath and slithered down with the water lapping under her chin. A little more of this and she would forget she had ever been chilled to the bone.

She needed a few days to recover from her trek through the White Mountains, but now she could relax so that when she went back to Christopher she would be glowing and radiant. She closed her eyes, letting her limbs move gently and sensuously, enjoying the feel of the little waves and currents eddying against her skin. Then she jumped out of the bath and began to towel herself so briskly that her damp pink skin was turning scarlet.

Dabbing would have dried her. The rooms were so warm she could have strolled around naked and dried off within minutes. What she was trying to do was rub away Rafe Drayford's touch. Lying there, dreaming, floating, her nerve-ends had started reliving how it was when his hands were stroking her, soothing away the stiffness and quickening something infinitely more dangerous.

She had only just escaped in time. It could take all the time she had left to recover from those days and nights when she had been much too close to the brother Christopher hated.

She was almost the youngest diner in the dining-room. Most of the others looked like prosperous retired couples, some of them probably wintering here, and when she seated herself alone she got polite smiles, tinged with curiosity.

She bought guidebooks and took them up to her room after dinner and began to plan. She should be phoning home, which meant Christopher, telling him where she was staying, and she would tomorrow or the next day, but not tonight.

Tonight she sat alone on her balcony. Beyond the gardens and the shingle of the beach she could see the glittering sea. There would be rocks out there and in daylight she might swim out. She had no urge to plunge into dark seas here. From now on she was living safely and the hotel swimming-pool could be all that she needed.

Next day she exchanged her flight ticket back home for one from Rhodes, changing at Athens. She would be returning a day earlier than she had planned but by then she knew that she would be ready to leave, although she was having a super holiday, and feeling marvellous.

That had its funny side because her fellow guests

seemed to have decided she was convalescing. She was pale and she could have been delicate, and the more motherly-looking of the ladies took to asking her how she was this morning. She always said fine and enquired after their health, and she wondered if they thought she was recovering, all alone, from a virus or a broken romance.

She didn't hang around in the hotel long enough to be questioned, and it amused her that if she had been honest with them she would have had to say, 'I'm getting over a collision with a mountain man.'

She hired a car and followed her guidebook, climbing the steep steps to the Acropolis, visiting churches, chapels, a medieval castle. But most of her time was spent in the old walled city of Rhodes. The crowds had gone and when the November rains came she could find herself in an almost deserted cobbled alley with perhaps just a woman in black hurrying ahead.

Some of the shops and tavernas were closed. She ate in others, enjoying the food and the company and dealing firmly with the passes that came her way. She bought shoes, a suit in a heavy tan silk, a couple of dresses and a swimsuit, a handbag and brooch for her mother, and bits of jewellery, ceramics and pottery for friends.

She was at a loss for Christopher. In the end she bought cufflinks, although she was sure he already had enough, and was looking into the window of an upmarket art gallery, for something that might be halfway suitable for Anna, when a canvas caught her eye.

She hadn't really examined Rafe's paintings. She hadn't had much chance, and she didn't know all that much about modern art so he could have made her feel a fool if he'd started talking about it. But something about this seascape reminded her of the colours and brushwork and vitality in his work that she must have glimpsed in passing.

When she went inside a grey-suited silver-haired man approached her and she pointed to the picture, quoting her guidebook vocabulary, '*Póso káni*?' When he told her the figure she staggered back, laughing, and he said,

'An investment.' Her accent must have told him she was English. He smiled too as she shook her head. She might not be buying but he seemed to have no doubts that a buyer would be turning up to take it off his hands, and he was helpful finding her a pretty little filigree box that Anna Drayford would probably drop into a drawer and forget.

During the last few days Caroline developed an attack of conscience about the cards she hadn't sent, and scribbled them to everyone who sent her cards when they were on holiday. They would arrive after she did, but cards from holidays abroad usually did. It was the thought that counted, even if hers had been belated.

She hadn't phoned anyone and by now that hardly seemed worthwhile. She would be there to answer questions in person, and to tell Christopher how much she had missed him and how she never wanted to go anywhere without him again.

She had a pleasant flight back; she felt rested and revived from her holiday, and there were no delays, no hitches at all. Her car was waiting where she had left it, in the airport car park, and she packed her cases and headed for home and Christopher.

She had begun the drive from the airport in high

spirits, but as the miles rushed by her mood began to change, until she was gripping the wheel so tightly that her knuckles whitened and a frown was cutting deep between her brows. And the nearer she came the stronger her uneasiness grew.

It's jet lag, she told herself, a stomach upset, a touch of malaise, and driving down the main road of her home town, with everything looking just as it had two weeks ago, should have reassured and settled her.

But her mouth was dry and her heart was hammering as she turned the car into the drive beside the shop that led to the garage in the yard at the back. As she unbuckled her seatbelt and opened the car door her mother came running from the side-door, and as Caroline jumped from the car Mary Hammond wailed, 'Where have you *been*?'

'You know where I've been. I've been to Crete. . . to Greece.'

'Nobody could get in touch with you. Christopher's been on to us and we didn't know—nobody knew—and he's very upset.'

Her parents would hate to have her upsetting Christopher, and maybe she had been thoughtless, but her usually placid mother sounded frantic, and Caroline asked, 'What has been happening?'

'Not what,' said Mary Hammond, 'who. His brother's come back. Rafe Drayford's here.'

# CHAPTER SIX

'RAFE can't be here,' gasped Caroline, although she knew that it would have been easy enough for anyone to travel from Crete in the time she had spent in Rhodes. What she meant was, I don't want him here; I've been running from him ever since I left the village. What she meant was, *Why?*

'Been here for the best part of a week,' her mother said. Although from her doleful expression Mary Hammond didn't think it had been the best part of anything. She went on, 'Christopher didn't expect you to be going off without him. That was a shock to him; that wasn't a very sensible thing to be doing.'

Caroline got her cases out of the boot. 'I told him I was going. It was a rush in the end, but I had told him.'

She left her car outside the garage and her mother followed her into the house, keeping her voice down because there were neighbours, customers, in the shop, and already there was gossip. 'Christopher wanted to know if we knew where you were staying, but we didn't. Nobody did. And then Rafe walks into the Grove.'

The side-door let into a little passage, one door connecting with the shop while another opened into the living-room and the kitchen. Closing the living-room door behind them, Mary said, 'You never said you were going to see Rafe Drayford while you were away.'

117

'I wasn't sure I was. His mother asked me to try to get a letter to him.'

'They never got on that well, those two,' said her mother. 'If you'd told us we'd have advised you to keep away from Rafe.'

She wouldn't have listened, but it would have been good advice. The best. She asked,

'Have you seen him?'

'Your father has—I wasn't in the shop. Very pleasant, your father said he was, but he could always charm ducks off water when he wanted to. He told your father you seemed to be enjoying your holiday. You were going shopping and sightseeing.'

'That's what I did,' said Caroline. 'His mother would be pleased to see him.'

'More than his brother is,' Mary said grimly. 'And who can blame him? Rafe Drayford always put Christopher in the shade.'

She was bothered and it was making her garrulous. Suddenly realising that what she was saying to Caroline was a tactless truth, she hurried on, 'But Christopher's a fine man. He's earned the right to be the heir and it would be a crying shame if Rafe came back and took it away from him. You gave him his mother's letter? She asked him to come home?'

'Yes.'

'Well,' and Mary Hammond sighed deeply, 'you'd have done better not to have gone looking for him because he's here and Christopher looks as if he's given up already, and whatever way you look at it you were the one who brought him home.'

'I did not bring him home,' said Caroline fiercely. 'Nobody brought him. And if he's decided to take over here Christopher had better start putting up a fight or

Rafe will ride roughshod over him, but he isn't rough-riding me.'

Mary Hammond's eyes widened, looking at her daughter. She had expected Caroline to be worried, but she had never before seen her blazing with anger.

Caroline had reason, of course, but if she stormed into Virginia Grove Anna and Robert Drayford would turn against her, and Mary said fearfully, 'You won't do anything. . .silly, will you?'

'I missed my chance,' said Caroline. 'I should have shoved him off a mountain.'

She took her cases up to her bedroom, her mother following again, asking, 'Shall I phone Christopher and tell him you're back? I promised I would as soon as we got any news of you.'

'I'll ring him,' said Caroline. 'It's been a long journey and I need to freshen up.'

She needed to be alone because this had been totally unexpected and traumatic, like one of those horror films where someone on the run reached somewhere that should have been safety at last, only to find the monster rearing up ahead.

Why *was* he here? Everything he had said had given her the impression that he was never coming back. Her mother thought he was back to stay. Caroline couldn't believe that, but she didn't *know*. She knew nothing, except that hearing that Rafe Drayford was almost within shouting distance was terrifying. She leaned against the bedroom door when her mother left the room, her back pressed hard against it as if she was at bay.

He had no right to come marching back into their well-ordered lives, upsetting everyone. He had opted out and he should damn well have stayed out. She was seething with righteous anger, bringing back the memory of striking him across the face. Nobody else made her violent. She had been confused then. Now her mind was clear, reason and instinct telling her that Rafe Drayford was out to wreck her peaceful existence and play havoc with the man she loved.

She began to unpack, delaying the time when she must come out of her room and face whatever was waiting; but she was still sorting out laundry when her mother opened the door to tell her, 'Christopher's here—I phoned him,' excusing herself, 'well, I did promise, and he was at home and he's come straight down.'

Christopher Drayford was in the little living-room, sitting on the edge of the sofa, looking towards the open door, waiting for Caroline; and at her first sight of him a wave of almost maternal tenderness filled her. He seemed so unhappy that she ran to throw her arms around him. They clung to each other, and she hated Rafe because nobody else could have made Christopher this wretched this quickly.

'It's all right,' she said. 'It's not the end of the world. So he's back, but he'll go away again, I'm sure he will, so it doesn't matter.'

'What happened? You found him, you gave him the letter.'

'He must have told you this.'

'He did.' Christopher took her hand and pulled her down to sit facing him while he scanned her features anxiously. 'What did he say to you?'

'About coming home? I didn't think he would but I must have got the wrong idea. He introduced me to some old men and women in the village who remembered my grandfather. He was in the White Mountains during the war.'

'Was he?' said Christopher, who knew nothing of Danni. 'How long were you with Rafe?'

'A couple of days. I wanted to go into the mountains and he's been there quite a while, so he acted as a guide. Most of the time I was in Rhodes.'

'You never phoned. Why didn't you phone?'

'Sorry.' She had not wanted to get in touch with anyone. She had been trying to get over Rafe Drayford as though he was a sickness, so that she could come home sound and sane to Christopher. And she had. Only to find that Rafe was here before her.

'Did he talk about me?' Christopher wanted to know.

'Not much. He asked about the folk around here but not about anyone in particular, not even Isabel. Did he just walk in?'

Christopher was beginning to relax, as if, with Caroline beside him, he might manage to stand up to his brother. 'Just turned up. When I got home from work last Tuessday my mother came running out, smiling, and said, "Such a surprise. Come and see what Caroline has done for us."'

Caroline said furiously, 'This is nothing to do with me. I didn't suggest his coming home. I didn't want him here. I never liked him in the old days and I don't like him any better now.'

Christopher held her face cupped in his hands and his voice was husky. 'I love you,' he said. 'You're beautiful and gentle and kind and I never wanted to let my brother near you. I must keep you away from him, I must.'

'I'll do that for myself,' she said. 'So he was here when you got home?'

'With my father. The old man was glad to see him, in spite of everything. He'd take him back into the firm, he'd take him back.' He looked at Caroline, begging for reassurance, although how could she know what Robert Drayford wanted?

She said, 'I don't think Rafe wants to be a lawyer again. He was painting. There were pictures.'

'He's having an exhibition in London.'

'Is he?' He had said nothing about his work when he was telling her about his travels. She suggested, 'Shall we take off for the evening? I'll tell you about my holiday and you can tell me what you've been doing, and we won't mention Rafe. We'll ignore him entirely.'

'Nobody ignores my brother,' Christopher said gloomily. 'All the years he's been away his shadow's still been over me. And now he's back, and I've got to take you up there because my mother took your mother's phone call and she's waiting to thank you for bringing the prodigal home.'

'She can thank me for nothing tomorrow,' said Caroline. 'I thought you wanted me to keep away from Rafe.'

'They're expecting us,' said Christopher as if there was no way out, and she wondered who scared him most, his brother or his parents, and could have shaken him. Then her impatience turned on herself because he was under so much pressure. Anyhow, her meeting Rafe again was unavoidable. She might as well get it over with.

'I've bought a present for your mother and you,' she said. 'If I'd known your brother was going to be here I'd have brought something for him, like strychnine.'

That got a faint grin from Christopher. 'I wouldn't put it past him to be able to drink strychnine and stay on his feet. He was always hard as nails and he's come back a world tougher than when he went away.' She didn't say, 'I know that', although she did.

She ran upstairs to fetch the little gifts and Christopher seemed thrilled with his cufflinks, which were nothing much. In fact he was going over the top in his gratitude and perhaps it was having Caroline home again, someone who was entirely on his side, that he was thankful for.

They went out by the side-door, passing the shop windows through which several customers peered, and in the background Caroline was sure her parents were watching.

The grounds of the Grove were on the outskirts of the village, the shop a few minutes' walk down the main road, and before Caroline and Christopher came to the lodge, and the tree-lined approach to the house, they had passed quite a few locals who had smiled and greeted them; and it seemed to Caroline that everyone had a wary look as if they would have liked to ask, 'Is he here to take over? Where does that leave you two?'

Set in immaculate green lawns and covered in the creeper that gave it its name, Virginia Grove had an ageless look. Caroline had begun to think of it as her future home. She loved it, and that was easy when it was such a beautiful house. So peaceful and perfect. But today there was a time bomb ticking away in there.

All the time she was thinking, I should never have gone to Crete. Somehow I have brought this trouble on us. Your mother's letter alone would not have done it.

Anna was waiting for Caroline as she had never

waited before, opening the main doors herself and greeting Caroline with misty eyes and outstretched hands. 'Bless you,' she said. 'How did you do it?'

Caroline drew back, missing the chance of being embraced so warmly by Christopher's mother, to protest, 'I did nothing. I gave him your letter, that's all.'

'Well,' said Anna gaily, 'it worked. Rafe's home. Come.' She took Caroline's hand, and Christopher's, and led them into the long drawing-room as if she was presenting them to somebody special, and it took all Caroline's self-control not to snarl, 'What does he expect, a curtsy?'

It *was* a long room, almost the length of the house, longer if you took in the conservatory, which threw green light through glass-panelled doors. It seemed to take ages to reach the far end of the room, where Rafe stood by the white marble fireplace, his father in a wingbacked chair beside him.

Robert Drayford had been laughing. Caroline had never heard him do much laughing before. He was a dignified, rather pompous man, but he was chuckling now and he went on smiling as the trio approached. What was there to laugh at? Caroline wanted to ask. She wanted to ask a lot of things, but it might be safer to keep her mouth shut. Only she didn't think she could manage that.

Out of mountain gear, Rafe was wearing a dark suit, impeccably cut, and what looked like a silk shirt and tie. 'Well, if it isn't the mountain man,' Caroline said. 'I didn't expect to be seeing you again so soon.'

'Home from the hills,' he said.

His hair was still the same length but groomed so that it seemed well cut, less wild. But his eyes hadn't changed; they were still dark and hooded. His smile was still amused and knowing, as if he saw the joke if she didn't. He was at home here, with the authority of a naturally powerful man, and the force of his personality was overwhelming.

Anna Drayford had seated herself, letting Caroline go, but Caroline was not taking Rafe's hand. She had the feeling that if he touched her this room and everything in it would dissolve and she would be high in the frozen hamlet again, a million miles from home.

She looked around, jerking her head, enquiring, 'Elpida with you?'

'No.'

'You do love 'em and leave 'em, don't you?'

'Don't *you*?' he said.

Was he talking about Christopher? She had never really left Christopher and she never would again. She reached to slide her hand through Christopher's arm and Christopher smiled at her. 'Oh, no,' she said.

'Did you have a lovely holiday?' Anna was asking her.

'Thank you, yes.'

'You're very pale.' Today Anna was solicitous about Caroline, who had the makings of a helpful daughter-in-law. And Caroline was looking wan, because she had had no time to colour her face before she was brought up here after the long flight home, and because seeing Rafe again was icing her blood.

'My lily-girl,' said Christopher, and Rafe burst out laughing and said,

'A charming flower. You can't beat lilies for purity.'

His lips were twitching, and Caroline fixed him with a level stare. 'Nice of you to say so. What changed your mind and brought you home?'

'Do I need a reason?'

'Of course you didn't,' said his mother. 'It was high time and we are all happy.'

She was. She had never looked at Christopher with the doting smile she was giving Rafe. And the old man, as Christopher called him, although Robert Drayford looked good for another twenty years, seemed to have forgotten the roaring rage of the last scene with his son.

Everything was forgiven now, as if Rafe was the son to be proud of instead of a man who had wasted his talents and was even conning free lodgings in the White Mountains. Caroline suspected that someone else had paid for that expensive suit he was wearing, because he had seemed flat broke to Caroline.

That must have been what brought him home. Letters were one thing, but a flesh and blood reminder of the old life would carry more weight. Her ruby ring was an heirloom—a plump Victorian lady wore it in an oil painting hanging in the dining-room. Seeing his brother's fiancée flaunting it, Rafe could have decided he should lay claim to some of the properties and possessions that had always been the birthright of the first-born male. There were rich pickings here wherever you looked.

She dug into her pocket and came up with the small packaged gift for Anna, which, like the cufflinks, was nothing compared with what she already had, but was, 'Just a thought,' Caroline said as she handed it over.

Anna opened the little shiny black bag with the gold lettering, unwrapping the leaves of tissue to reveal what could be a pillbox or a ringbox. The filigree was a delicate floral tracery and Anna said it was quite enchanting and kissed Caroline warmly. Again Caroline knew she was getting more appreciation than her gifts warranted. Rafe Drayford's mother was thanking her because Rafe was here. Right now Caroline could do no wrong, and she felt like screaming, *NO*. . .because she would have paid almost every penny she had to have kept him away.

Anna had dropped the bag on a low table beside her chair and Rafe bent over to pick it up, reading the name. 'Nikos of Rhodes! Small world.'

'A friend of yours?' his mother asked.

'He started as a dealer but he's a friend now.'

'He sells your pictures?' Caroline squeaked.

'Yes.'

She stopped herself from gasping like a landed fish. She hadn't thought anyone was selling them. She had thought they were just piling up around the house, but that was a very superior gallery, and that painting in the window—suddenly she was sure it was Rafe's—had had pride of place.

Christopher said, 'Sell well, don't they?' and Caroline thought they must sense the bitterness. But Robert Drayford was beaming like a man who had been brought good news and couldn't hear it too often, and his wife said blithely,

'*Very* well. Isn't that splendid? He's had exhibitions in Athens and Paris, and now he's getting pictures together for one in London, which will probably go on to New York.'

'I don't believe it,' said Caroline, managing to make that sound like polite surprise. 'Why has nobody heard about this?'

Again Anna answered, this time with mock severity, 'Because he didn't use his full name. He uses Michali. He's Rafe Michael Drayford.' She tutted at her son.

'Well, everybody's going to know now that we've got a successful artist in the family.'

Caroline said stupidly, 'That makes a change,' because they seemed to expect her to say something.

She felt no better for this news. Even a successful artist's future was chancy, so this didn't mean Rafe had no designs on Christopher's inheritance, and being successful would go a long way to get him back into his parents' good books. He hadn't come home like some New Age Traveller, he'd come back with kudos and clout and they would already be boasting about him to their friends.

'You left something behind in the White Mountains,' said Rafe, and she held her breath at that gleam of laughter in his eyes. The oil-soaked undies! How was she going to explain that? She would have to tell them what had happened, of the stiffness, so that she had oiled her joints. But she would flatly deny that she was almost naked while Rafe had been applying the oil. She would lie through her teeth, and now she bared her teeth in a passable semblance of a smile.

'You brought whatever it was for me? All this way?'

'Of course.' He was taking a wallet out of his pocket and producing a sketch of Danni. She had realised in Rhodes that she had left that behind with Giorgio and been sorry about it. She was so glad to get it back that she hardly begrudged him his little game of cat-and-mouse, but it showed her the way things were going. He was amusing himself here, and if he decided he wanted a real laugh there could be no holds barred.

She showed them the sketch and explained, and Robert asked about the men and women who had known Caroline's grandfather, neighbours of Rafe's in the mountains. Anna asked, 'Is Elpida from the village?'

'Yes,' said Rafe.

'Who is she?' His mother was more interested in a girl he might have brought home with him than in the old freedom fighters.

'A good friend of mine,' he said.

Ha! thought Caroline, and said, 'A very beautiful friend,' and could have gone on, out to embarrass him as he was embarrassing her if she could, but the hardening of his mouth shut her up like a hand clapped over her own mouth. She was not afraid of him, but he was dangerous.

'Well, she would be, wouldn't she?' Christopher muttered, and Anna smiled and began to talk to Caroline.

'We must have a welcome-home party for Rafe, and we've never had a real celebration of your engagement.'

It seemed to Caroline that all sorts of fuss had been made. She and Christopher had gone together to parties galore where everybody had congratulated them, and she had helped Anna hostess gatherings at the Grove. But perhaps there had not been an engagement party.

'In two or three weeks' time,' Anna went on. 'Maybe the week before Christmas.'

Caroline passed a strange hour in the long drawing-room that night. She was used to this room now, as much at home here as she was in the little sitting-room behind the shop. More at home, maybe. Every piece of furniture, every picture on the walls was familiar to her, and since she had had the ruby ring on her finger she had been one of the family, one of the Drayfords.

But Rafe Drayford changed all that. He stood by the fireplace, while everyone else was seated, and they all looked towards him and the conversation was for him. As if he was controlling them all, Caroline thought sourly.

She tried to lean back in her chair and keep her distance but she was edgy tonight, as if she had not been accepted at all but was here on approval. The talk was mostly about the years before Rafe had cleared off and before Caroline had moved in, and she could have sworn he was emphasising this.

When names and places that meant nothing to her came up he would look at her as if she should be taking the cue, although he must know she had nothing to say. He cross-questioned her about her interests and her hobbies, as though she had told him nothing about herself before.

She hadn't told him much but now she found herself giving grudging replies, like trying to explain why she couldn't ride. There were horses in the stables and she enjoyed giving them carrots, or watching them in the paddock and seeing somebody else gallop off on them. But since Christopher had tried to teach her to ride she had taken a couple of painful falls and never become an addict.

'You ride, of course,' Rafe said, and she said flatly, 'Not very well.'

'A pity. Chris is a good horseman.'

Christopher had been riding all his life but it was Rafe who had been the steeplechaser. His mother probably still had the cups and rosettes hidden away somewhere. She could be bringing them out again now, and Caroline said sweetly, 'I know he is, but he doesn't mind that I'm not. We have so much else in common.'

'Such as?' Rafe enquired, and that was sheer imper-
tinence, but he asked with a smile that could have
disarmed anyone but Caroline.

Anna said happily, 'Caroline is the daughter we've
always wanted,' and Christopher said,

'More than you'll ever know.'

'I couldn't be more pleased for you both,' said Rafe,
and if he didn't stop this Caroline would be asking
about Elpida. . . Are you going back to the girl you're
sleeping with or have you paid her off, as you seem to
be in the money?

She was biting her tongue because she must not
make a scene in front of Christopher's parents. Then a
phone rang, a business call that took both Christopher
and his father out of the room, and Anna got up and
said, 'I'll see about some coffee.'

Within seconds Caroline was alone with Rafe.
Nobody was listening, and she jumped to her feet and
hissed, 'Stop baiting me.' Then when she thought he
was starting to laugh she looked round wildly, and
froze in horror because she was looking for something
to throw, to smash. He could do that to her, blow her
mind, and she ran from the room, opening the glass
doors of the conservatory, getting away before she did
something that nobody but Christopher would ever
forgive.

The huge conservatory was Victorian, hot and humid
and full of greenery. Caroline reached the white
scrolled-iron seats under the palm trees, sat down,
breathing deeply, and waited. She was almost sure
Rafe would follow her, and if he asked if she was all
right she would scream.

He didn't ask that and she did not scream, but he

did follow. He indicated one of the chairs and asked, 'May I?' and she said,

'They're your chairs,' which was not quite true but near enough.

He sat down. 'Nothing much has changed,' he said. 'You could still suffocate in here.'

'After the White Mountains this must be a shock to your system,' she muttered.

'I'll adapt.' He looked as cool as ever. She felt that if she touched his face her fingers would freeze and then burn. He said, 'You were shocked to find me here.'

'I was surprised.'

'You were furious. You came down that room with a smile that looked as if it had been pinned on your face and was drawing blood. And you're not too pleased to hear that the paintings sell. Now why should that worry you?'

He wouldn't understand or care, but she would tell him why. She leaned forward, gripping the arms of the iron chair as if she was holding herself back. Her quiet voice shook a little because she wanted to shout.

'Like Christopher said, they would sell, wouldn't they, because everything you touch goes right? Everything happens the way you want it. You've always been a winner. Christopher works so hard and he still can't win when you're around. Your mother's drooling over you and your father's carrying on as if you're the only son he needs, and it isn't fair that everything should always come to you, and that it's no sweat, always so easy.'

That was how Christopher felt, how she did too. She was gasping, and the word 'easy' hung in the air, the ultimate accusation that summed up all her resentment.

He echoed it. 'Easy?' The dark face was mask-like with no emotion showing. He sat back, elbow on the arm of his chair, chin in hand. His voice was clipped and cold when he said, 'Nothing has come easily. I have been fighting all my life. But you couldn't understand that when the hardest thing you ever did was climb a mountain roped to me.'

Suddenly he reached towards her and she shrank back, but he caught her left hand. 'Getting this on your finger was probably easy enough. Come back and find a girl like Caroline, my mother said, and girls like Caroline are not hard to find, but you happened to be in the right place at the right time. *That* I call easy.'

He held her hand at arm's length as if he was admiring the ring. 'This has been around a while. I'm sure Chris has shown you old Harriet wearing it. Second from the left as you go into the dining-room. There's a plaque to her in the church—we're a great family for plaques. Harriet Drayford, beloved wife of William Drayford MP. She kept a journal all about her good works. On the sanctimonious side, but a worthy old biddy.'

He dropped her hand as if he was done with the ring and Caroline, and she wanted to raise her own hand and press it against her cheek for comfort, but it would have been too dramatic and she let her hand lie, although the ruby ring still glittered.

She said, 'I'd like to read her journal,' for something to bridge the silence.

'There are stacks of them. Anna probably keeps one herself. The Drayford wives don't have much literary talent but they do keep the records straight.'

She thought, Not everybody has your restless energy. Men like Christopher, women like me, are content to live quiet lives with time to stand and stare, and even write diaries.

Rafe Drayford was a man apart. He had no place in their lives, and she asked, 'What *are* you doing here?'

The mask had gone when he grinned at her. 'You remember the bet: if you got to the hamlet I'd come to your wedding.'

She had almost forgotten that, and of course it wasn't why she had been so obsessed with reaching the hamlet. The last thing she had wanted was to see him again. She said, 'I told you we were getting married in the spring.'

'I got it wrong.'

She thought, No, you did not. You have the kind of mind that remembers. 'Rubbish,' she said, and he smiled again.

'I do have an exhibition coming up in London, I am due over here, and there was no reason why I shouldn't see my folk. Getting my mother's letter and hearing you talk about people I used to know tipped the balance. I hadn't planned to come back, but why not?'

Why not? His parents were happier for seeing him. If only he didn't look so much the master, as if he had the strength and the right to take over, and what he was saying wasn't reassuring.

'There's something about this place. Walking around the house, the grounds, the village, riding over the hills. Maybe droit de seigneur means caring for your own.'

That sounded alarming and she licked dry lips before she could say, 'I won't let you take everything away from Christopher.'

'How would you go about stopping me?' and again anger rose in her until the blood was pounding in her ears. 'People in glass houses should not throw stones,' he said, so she must be looking as furious as she felt. Then he said, 'I'm not here to take anything from Christopher.'

'Thank heaven for that,' she blurted out, and his smile was cynical.

'It wouldn't make him such a catch, would it, if he was the also-ran?'

Her face flamed and she said through gritted teeth, 'I will not lose my temper. You make me so angry that I don't recognise myself.'

She hated the wildness he unleashed in her, the something in his voice or manner or vibes that ripped her control to shreds. She had to keep control, and she glared at him in silence.

'I don't know about you being the lily-girl,' he said. 'A tiger-lily might be more like it,' and she snapped,

'I wish I were a tiger—I'd be better fitted for dealing with you.'

'I'll say it again,' he said, 'you could be the death of Christopher. He wouldn't recognise you now. Nor would Anna. This isn't the daughter she always wanted and I'm damn sure it isn't the wife Christopher thinks he's getting.'

'Who cares what you think?'

'They all do.'

It looked that way, but she said, '*Ha!*' aloud this time, a derisory hoot. 'Not Christopher. He wouldn't believe anything you told him.'

'We'll see,' said Rafe Drayford.

He was too big for these chairs. His long legs stretched across the black and white tiled floor, ankles crossed. His broad shoulders blocked out the iron-scrolled back of the chair, while Caroline had room to wriggle, getting hotter by the minute. She sat still, trying not to squirm, demanding, 'What are you going to tell him? What can you?'

He shrugged. 'I don't know yet. What I do know is that, having come back, I'm feeling a responsibility. I want things right for them here.'

'You said I was right for Christopher.'

'Perhaps you are.' She could not believe that she was discussing if she should be wearing Christopher's ring with someone who had probably never given Christopher a thought in years. 'But I'm beginning to have doubts. Christopher needs all the steady support he can get. You can be an exhausting woman.'

'I can be exhausting?' She jabbed a forefinger towards herself. '*Me*? Compared with you I'm a mill-pond against a force eight gale. And how much support have you ever given him? You've always made him feel second-best.'

'Then it's time I made amends and started looking out for him,' and she howled,

'Just leave us alone, won't you? We're fine.'

'I'll go,' he said, 'when I'm satisfied that my brother isn't heading for the mistake of his life.'

'Mistakes, is it? The first mistake was the letter. My mistake was finding you, and your mistake is thinking you're going to sit in judgement on me.'

'That's exactly what I'm doing,' he said and his arrogance rendered her speechless so that she could only gulp, tasting acid but unable to spit it out, while Anna Drayford's dulcet tones floated across.

'Hello, coffee's here. . .are you there?'

'Here we are,' Rafe called back.

Anna came to find them, talking gaily all the way,

and he sat watching Caroline as she struggled to compose herself before Anna reached them.

By the time Anna had appeared Caroline was smiling nicely, remembering what he had said about her earlier smile, feeling that this was much the same, false and painful. But it was fooling Anna, who seemed pleased to see Rafe and Caroline getting along so well.

It was lovely having Rafe home, thought Anna. She loved Christopher, of course, but Rafe was so much stronger, a man who could deal with anything. She smiled at him so proudly that Caroline believed that if he had told her, 'Caroline Hammond won't do for Christopher,' Anna Drayford would have listened to him, prepared to be persuaded.

And if Rafe turned his parents against her they would soon have her out of their home and even out of Christopher's life.

## CHAPTER SEVEN

THIS is a crazy idea, Caroline told herself. Rafe Drayford couldn't really care who Christopher married, although right now he was amusing himself putting Christopher's fiancée into a panic. Well, she was not panicking but she could have a fight on her hands.

She looked straight at Rafe, and the clashing of their eyes was like a physical impact that jarred her spine. When he stood up her head went back, their gazes still locked, but when he held out a hand to her she jumped to her feet, avoiding his touch.

Anna Drayford, a few steps ahead, was talking about the house plants. Most of them had been here for years—Rafe must have been reared with them—and her voice was like an insect's buzzing to Caroline, who was irritated to near screaming pitch because Rafe had a hand under her elbow, guiding her. She didn't need guiding. This wasn't a rainforest, although it felt hot and damp enough for one.

When she stepped into the drawing-room and cooler air Christopher and his father were just coming back into the room, but Rafe still held her arm, and as she jerked it away he enquired, 'How's the stiffness?'

'Long gone.'

Christopher looked puzzled. His father said jovially, 'Taking a turn round the hothouse?'

'It is hot in there,' Anna agreed. 'It's put some colour into Caroline's cheeks.'

Caroline's flaming face was caused by anger, but she

had to smile and join Anna dispensing coffee and sit and listen to Robert Drayford telling Rafe about the phone call just now. She looked anywhere except at Rafe, because that was the only way she could calm down.

The call had been connected with a complicated company trust, double Dutch to Caroline, and when Robert Drayford told Rafe, 'We've missed you. There's always an opening for you with the old firm,' Caroline saw Christopher wince.

She said quietly to Christopher, 'I should be going home. I walked straight out up here as soon as I got back and I've things to do.'

'I'll see you home.' She knew he wanted to get out of the room. Everybody said goodbye for now and she managed her goodbyes without meeting Rafe's eyes.

Out of the house dusk was falling; it was going to be a chilly night. The grounds of Virginia Grove were the size of a small park, and tonight they seemed cold and empty as Christopher and Caroline walked down the tree-lined avenue in silence, until Christopher burst out, 'You heard that? The old man's hellbent on keeping him here.'

'He won't stay,' she said.

'Another thing. . .' Christopher was not comforted '. . . he was a good lawyer, he's got a brilliant mind, and the estate has always gone in a direct line, always to the eldest son. He could root through old papers and find an entailment clause.'

'That's not very likely.' It seemed most unlikely and she said again, 'He won't stay,' adding, 'He's got to be free.'

Christopher turned to look into her face as they

walked towards her father's shop. 'You know him that
well, do you?' and she was frowning.

'I don't really know him at all, but I know that.'

They said goodnight outside the side-door. She
didn't ask him in, as she was travel-stained and tired.
She wanted to go in to work tomorrow and he would
drive her into town in the morning and pick her up at
lunchtime. He had a meeting locally, which should end
around midday.

'See you at half-eight,' he said and kissed her, and
she hugged him and said,

'Don't *worry*.' But she knew that he would, and this
was hardly the time to tell him that Rafe was contem-
plating saving him from Caroline.

Her mother and father were as worried as
Christopher, and she heard herself repeating what she
had said to him. 'It's all right, he won't stay; he doesn't
want Virginia Grove. It seems,' she said, 'that he's
doing very well as an artist,' and her father, who had
never been in an art gallery in his life, said
lugubriously,

'No money in pictures. What else has he come back
for, if it isn't to remind them he's in line for the lion's
share?'

Caroline's mother gave a little cry of protest,
although it was the way all her friends and neighbours
were thinking, and Caroline said, 'Don't *worry*,' and
went upstairs to fetch the gifts she had brought them.
'I don't want to hear another word about Rafe
Drayford tonight,' she said.

Over supper she told them about Rhodes, and her
mother told her some local gossip—nothing compared
to what was happening at the Grove, but it passed the
time. Nobody mentioned Rafe Drayford but he could

have been sitting at their table, he was such a real and disturbing presence.

Caroline couldn't have sworn she didn't dream of him. She woke early after a troubled night and his dark face could have been imprinted on her closed eyelids, because she saw him with her eyes shut and sat up, shaking her head, trying to clear her mind.

She needed to go in to work where she would be busy, dealing with matters that had nothing to do with the Drayfords. She waited for Christopher, and as soon as his car drew up she was out of the shop door and into the passenger seat, dodging a woman on the pavement, who said, 'Hello, you're back, then?'

'Looks like it,' Caroline beamed at her through the window although if the woman had noted Christopher's glum face it would have interested her even more than Caroline's smile.

Her parents had not been smiling either, and they were anxious and Christopher was anxious and Caroline was sorry for them all, but it wasn't a funeral. She said wearily, 'Oh, do cheer up,' and Christopher turned on the radio, apparently not feeling equal to cheery talk.

When they reached the suburbs of the town where she worked Caroline said, 'I'm sorry, I know it's rotten for you. Anything else happened?'

Christopher sighed. 'The way they're all carrying on you'd think he'd won the Nobel peace prize and the Ashes.' Caroline giggled, but he wasn't being funny, he was whingeing, 'Guess who phoned this morning?'

She nearly made some wild, ridiculous guess although it wouldn't have lightened the situation, as

Christopher was sunk in gloom. But he didn't give her the chance to say anything. 'Isabel,' he said.

'Isabel Faulkner?' There was only one Isabel in Rafe's life so far as Caroline knew. 'I thought she was married.' She had heard that mentioned. She had never met Isabel.

'Can't be working out,' said Christopher. 'Seems she can't wait to take up with Rafe again.'

They were now into the main square, drawing up in front of Caroline's place of work, a mellowed brick building, the paintwork white, and the windows displaying couture models. Rafe hadn't wanted Isabel. She had bored him in the old days but he might feel differently about her now, and some of Christopher's gloom must have rubbed off on Caroline because suddenly she was feeling snappish.

'Thanks,' she said. 'See you for lunch.' Then she got out of the car before she could say, Someone ought to be warning the girl, stopping her making a fool of herself again. Rafe will eat her for breakfast, and you too if you don't get your act together.

She stood on the pavement for a moment, as if she didn't know which way to turn. A bitter little wind was blowing; there was snow in the air. Then one of the staff spotted her and the door was flung open. She was back a day early but they were pleased to see her and dying to hear the news from Virginia Grove.

None of them came from the village but they knew Rafe Drayford was home, and Sally had seen him in town here with Mrs Drayford a couple of days ago and thought he was devastating. With Caroline engaged to his younger brother there was the promise of high drama and they clustered around, waiting to be thrilled and shocked.

Caroline shrugged. 'He's having an exhibition of his paintings in London. He's come over about it. Then he'll be off again.' She hoped, and it sounded reasonable. 'Everybody all right here?' she asked.

They hadn't had their cards from Rhodes but she handed out the gifts, and by that time the shop was open and customers were strolling in.

Among the deliveries Sally had held back a wedding-dress. Caroline's dress was coming from here, of course, and this was a beauty in heavy ivory silk. It was hanging in Caroline's office and when she was through with the items in her in-tray she might try it on.

She did some phoning, some dictating. A snarl-up over a delayed delivery took surprisingly long to sort out. She was expecting Christopher when she finally put down the phone on that, and then she got up and went across to lift down the dress and stand in front of a long mirror, holding it against her.

Sally's neat dark head came round the door. 'Caller for you.'

'Send him in,' said Caroline.

'You're the boss.' Sally sounded as if she was smiling broadly and Caroline turned from the mirror as Rafe walked in, and Sally stepped back behind him, rolling her eyes and mouthing, 'Wow!'

He took stock of Caroline and the dress. 'Very lily-like,' he said, and she turned to hang it back, deciding there and then that it was not for her, demanding,

'What are you doing here?'

'Chris was held up, so I'm collecting you.'

Christopher would not have sent Rafe, but if Rafe had offered Christopher could hardly have refused. And the door was open and it was not only Sally who was hanging around outside. So Caroline had to get

into her coat, pick up her shoulder bag and walk out of
the shop with him. Staff and customers watched them
leave and started a chorus of chatter as soon as the
shop door closed.

When Christopher met her for lunch they usually ate
in the hotel across the square. It was convenient and
the food was good. She said, 'That's where Christopher
and I usually have lunch,' and without turning to look
he said,

'No, thanks.'

'I wasn't suggesting you take me out to lunch.' She
hadn't been. She had just been saying the first thing
that came into her head. 'Although it would have been
our first civilised meal, given you a chance to check if I
know which fork to use.'

'I know you're a dab hand with a hunting knife.'

'Is that what it was?' She grimaced. 'I'd have used
fingers if I'd known.'

His car was a sleek grey BMW parked in a side-
street. As he opened the door for her she said, 'Bought,
borrowed or stolen?' and he grinned.

'Oh, I can go to this.'

'From the price I was quoted for one of your
paintings in Nico's, I guess you can. The seascape in
the window is yours?'

'Yes.'

She grinned too. 'I should have tried to buy one off
you cheap.'

'Why didn't you?'

'Too late now, I suppose?' She ought to be keeping
her distance in every way, but being near him stimu-
lated her like a charge of adrenalin. When he had
walked into her little office the centrally heated air had
seemed fresh and sharp.

'Come to my exhibition and I'll give you a painting,' he said.

'For a wedding present?' She didn't know why she had said that. He turned to look at her and she should not meet his eyes because this time it was how it had been in the shepherd's hut, as if she was being drawn into whirling darkness. Then he looked away from her, switched on the ignition, and the car surged smoothly and powerfully forward.

Outside everyone was dressed for winter. Tiny flakes of snow were drifting down and they all walked along the pavement huddled against the chill. He smiled. 'They don't know what cold is, do they?'

'They have no idea.' These crowded streets and busy shops were a different world from the frozen hamlet in the mountains. But the man beside her lived in both worlds. At home wherever he was, travelling alone.

She said very casually, 'Christopher said Isabel phoned this morning.'

'Did she?' That seemed to surprise him.

'And she can't wait to take up with you again.'

'News to me,' he said, and she rocked with laughter.

'Well, well, I wonder who took that call. You should be sorting out your own love-life before you start on your brother's.'

'Mine is sorted out.'

'Love them and leave them.' She was still laughing, and the rest of the short journey passed more or less in silence. But easily enough. If he was being agreeable she was not out for a fight, and maybe this was a truce.

Driving through the village, nearing the shop, she said, 'Thanks for the lift; you can put me down here,' but he didn't slacken speed, and when she looked surprised he said,

'I'm not abducting you.'

'Wrong country, wrong girl.'

'But we should talk. About you and Christopher.'

There was nothing to discuss there, but she said, 'Why not?' and sat back in her seat until he stopped the car in the forecourt of Virginia Grove. The light snowfall was over, leaving a white powdering on the lawns like sugar on a cake. All the windows in the house seemed dark, and when they got out of the car they began to walk across the frozen grass, away from the wide steps that led to the main door. They walked apart but she could feel him beside her as though little currents ran between them.

He asked, 'Do we still have the fête here?'

The traditional church fête was still held at Virginia Grove. She and her mother had always helped on some stall or other, but this year she had walked around with the Drayfords. The weather had been good, it had been as successful as ever and only a few months ago. But somehow the recent memory was less vivid than that day, nearly five years ago, when she had been a schoolgirl and Rafe Drayford had been part of his family for the last time.

'The tombola was there,' he said.

'That was where I was.' They were rounding the house now. 'I thought you were going to make a bolt for it then,' she said.

Isabel had been clutching his arm; Elpida clung on to him too; and Caroline dug her hands into her pockets in case she should forget herself and link up with him. She said, 'You looked like someone who had been almost caged but not quite,' and burst out laughing.

'That was exactly how it was.' Formal gardens led

off the lawns, a tennis court, a rose arbour, an avenue
of boxed hedges ending in a low mound topped by a
gazebo. He looked up towards the gazebo. 'There was
always a fortune-teller in there.'

'Still the same one. Mrs Dunn from the bakery in
gypsy costume and greasepaint. As she knows everybody's business she shouldn't go far wrong. Did she
tell your fortune.'

Anna Drayford always shepherded her family, like
minor royalty, from stall to stall and the fortune-teller's
was no exception. 'She told me I'd found true love and
was heading for a rosy future,' he said. 'What did she
see for you? Or were you too busy on the tombola?'

'We always have our fortunes told. That year she
said I'd get my A levels and I did. This year I got true
love and the rosy future.' This year Caroline had been
engaged to Christopher Drayford and everyone at the
fête thought her future was made.

'No mention of the White Mountains? And a dark
stranger?'

'Not a word.'

'Mine didn't say much for her psychic powers either,
considering I was near-suicidal at the time.'

They laughed together. He took her hand and they
climbed the steps to the gazebo, a square brick building
with a pointed roof, windows and door overlooking the
avenue. Inside old blue and white Dutch tiles lined the
walls and covered a wide waist-high shelf. There was
no furniture but in Victorian days, when picnics had
been all the rage, chairs and baskets would have been
brought from the house, and food and drink kept cool
on the tiled slabs.

It was chilly enough in here today to cool off any
picnic, but they closed the door behind them and

looked down through the windows over the empty avenue. Caroline said, 'I've always liked it in here.'

'It was one of my bolt holes; I used to come out here to sketch.' Nobody else knew that, she was sure, and she wanted to hear more.

'What did you sketch?'

He grinned with cheerful malice. 'I was a fair hand at caricatures. When I was tempted to knock somebody down I came in here and knocked them off instead, if you'll pardon the expression. Look,' he picked her up bodily and before she had time to do more than gasp he had seated her on the slab a little further along from where she had been standing, 'these four tiles could be lifted—I used to hide my stuff in here.'

She was digging into her bag, coming up with a nail-file. He shrugged obligingly and slid it into the thin dark gap between the tiles, lifting one carefully. But when he took it out, and the one beside it, and she peered into the space beneath, it was empty, and she wailed, 'There's nothing there.'

'I destroyed them before I left. I'd said all I needed to say.'

If they had come across the cache later it would have been wounding. He had considered their pride a little, but she said, 'I'd like to have seen just one,' and he offered,

'Tell me somebody you dislike and I'll sketch them for you.'

'How about a self-portrait?' But there was no venom in this, this was fooling, and she said, 'Talking about old papers, Christopher is worried that you might find something called—is it an entailment, about the eldest son always inheriting?'

'Is there one?' He didn't sound that interested.

'He doesn't know. He's just scared there might be. It would be way, way back.'

'If there was I'm not looking for it.' He might not need to. His father would hand over to him if he stayed, and she asked,

'Did you always want to get away?'

'Almost as long as I can remember. Boarding-school and Cambridge were all right—I could more or less think for myself there. Back here I *was* caged, with every aspect of my life mapped out for as long as I lived.'

His voice had been quiet, musing. Suddenly it became sharp and searching. 'You'll like that, will you?'

It would be a wonderful life; everybody said so. She nodded mutely, and he went on, 'It will suit Christopher. Is that one of the things you have in common?'

'It is.' It was.

'And what else?'

'*No!*'

'Can't you think of anything else?' He could be teasing in friendly fashion, but she was suddenly unsure what he was doing, and she said,

'I certainly can. We have the same tastes in most things, we enjoy being together, we love each other.'

'How's the sex?' he said abruptly and she had to swallow before she could manage the right nonchalant note.

'On a scale of one to ten, at least nine and a half.'

'Not good enough.'

This was dangerous talk, and she was having no more of it. 'More than good enough,' she said, 'and I must be getting home.' But he stood in front of her, putting both his hands flat on the wall behind her, so that there was no way she could slither off the slab.

'Compared to what?' he enquired gently, and she panted,

'Let me get down. Who the hell do you think you are?'

'I know who I am. Who are you, behind that *Mona Lisa* calm? You can snarl and bite—have you ever lashed out at Christopher?'

She was horrified. 'Of course not,' and he mimicked her horror.

'Of course not. Or he'd have been running for cover.'

Here it came again, the almost uncontrollable rage. Again she clenched her jaw, forcing the words through her teeth. 'I have never lashed out at anyone but you. I can't remember ever snapping at anyone before. Nobody, but nobody, makes me so angry.'

He didn't move a muscle, leaning over her as she leaned away, the small of her back pressed against the smooth tiles of the wall. 'So you've said. You're how old? Twenty-two? Twenty-three? And I'm the first you've lost your temper with?'

She had had a placid life; she had thought she had a placid nature. She croaked, '*Yes*!' and now she sounded as if hands were round her throat, letting only a whisper get through.

But his voice was as calm as if he was summing up a case as a lawyer. 'A first for rage, so something about me gets under your skin—that proves you're alive in there. What else can we reach?'

Face to face his arms were hard and straight, boxing her in as if there was no air or space in the world beyond him. While he held her here her every muscle was tense and rigid so that she could neither move nor speak.

Then his palms slipped from the wall and his hands were behind her. She could feel them on her shoulder blades, down her spine, like the time in the hamlet, warming her blood. And quickening a hunger so that her face was pressed against his cheek. Her eyes were closed tight and he kissed her eyelids, then her closed lips until they softened and parted, letting his tongue take her tongue, all of her melting.

Her head dropped back so that it hit the wall, and he cradled it in his hand, rocking her. She felt him shudder and she shuddered too. 'Hush,' he said, 'hush,' and somehow she moaned,

'No,' opening her eyes to the trap she was in.

She must have struggled because suddenly he was no longer holding her. He was standing back, eyes hooded, smiling the crooked smile. 'We do find ourselves in some uncomfortable settings,' he said.

Against a tiled slab. On a frozen floor up a mountain. Both times she had been transported out of her surroundings until she hadn't known where she was. Or cared. She hardly knew now, the blue and white tiles were blurring, and as she edged off the shelf she turned to hold on to it for support. 'I must go,' she said.

He said nothing. He was there, tall and strong, and she had to walk away steadily or he would take her arm, or even pick her up, and she could hang on to him and that would be the end of everything.

She walked from the gazebo, down the steps, down the avenue, heart and head thumping. That was a ferocious pass, she supposed. Or perhaps it didn't turn ferocious until she responded. She had responded and it was no surprise that she fancied Rafe Drayford. He stirred all sorts of reactions in her: dislike, distrust, excitement, lust. Some in her mind, some in her body, all of them dangerous. Just walking along with him now was making her skin tingle.

If he was against Christopher's marrying her he had something to tell. Although what could he say? I kissed the girl wearing your ring. She said no and that was it. . .a flare of passion and a seduction that stopped short.

The house loomed ahead of them and he said casually, 'Coming in for lunch?'

He didn't seem to think anything ferocious had occurred. But it had, in her mind. She had nearly gone tiger-wild, but not quite, thank her lucky stars, and by now she had her voice steady too. She could ask, 'Who else is for lunch?' with the right lightness, and when he said,

'Nobody but me,' she could say,

'Thanks, but no.'

'I'm not going to drag you into the bedrooms.'

They were fooling again and she made a shocked face. 'I wonder how Mrs Green would react to that.' Mrs Green was the cook. There would be staff in the house, and of course Rafe Drayford and Christopher's fiancée would not end up in a bed.

'How would you react?'

'I bite and claw.'

'That you do.'

She said, 'I'm going home, and for the record, from now on I'm keeping away from you.'

She walked fast across the lawns, the grass crunching under her feet. When he called, 'Caroline,' she turned her head without pausing. 'You're welcome to try,' he said, and she kept on walking.

She had to keep away from him. He was invading her mind, day and night, and she carried the memory of his touch deep in her skin. Just now she had come close to a bonding from which she would never have escaped. She had to keep telling herself that she loved Christopher, and she did, but Rafe Drayford could scare her to death. She *had* to keep away. . .

Back home she busied herself, preparing the evening meal. Her father had taken the van to the cash-and-carry to collect stock; her mother was behind the counter in the shop. Caroline peeled potatoes, having carefully removed her ring before she put her hands into water. She couldn't handle the peeler in rubber gloves but it would have been awful if any of the stones had worked loose from the antique setting, and when she dried her hands and reached for the ring again she hesitated. For a moment she was not sure that she wanted to go on wearing it.

It was a beautiful ring; she was proud of it and of what it stood for. Not the status or the Drayford holdings, but Christopher, who was her own dear love. But while she thought of Christopher she could feel Rafe Drayford beside her, his breath or his fingers stirring her hair. She was desperately trying to think of Christopher, but Rafe was *here*. Or might as well have been.

She put on the ring and went to the phone and dialled the local office branch where Christopher was based today. He was still out and she left a message that she was home. He would ring her here, and while she waited for his call she washed her hair and experimented with different styles in front of her dressing-table mirror.

In the end she would stay with the style she had,

smooth dark waves swept back from her pale face, but this was something to do, some sort of action, trying out a different image. 'Who are you?' Rafe had said, and her personality seemed to be splintering. She had never been so confused, in such turmoil.

When the phone rang she ran downstairs and snatched up the receiver as her mother came through the door from the shop. It was the voice she was waiting for. 'Christopher,' she said, and Mary Hammond smiled and retreated.

He was sorry he had not got away earlier but the meeting had dragged. Rafe had collected her, had he? 'Oh, yes,' she said.

Rafe had looked in on the meeting, said Christopher. He knew all of them there and had delayed things further, and then he had said he would collect Caroline.

'That was kind of him,' she said tartly.

'No problems?' He sounded anxious.

If she had said, He tried to seduce me in the gazebo, they would all have had problems. 'No,' she said.

'What did he talk about?'

He had asked how sex was between them, and she wished she had given it full marks then he couldn't have said, 'Not good enough.' 'Nothing much,' she said. 'Can we go out somewhere tonight, just the two of us? How about the Golden Partridge? I could see if I could book a table.'

'I'd like nothing better,' Christopher said. He was phoning from the open-plan office—she could hear background sounds and voices—and Christopher was easily embarrassed, so that when he said fervently, 'I love you,' she was touched.

She said, 'Thank you, and I'm dotty about you.'

The Golden Partridge was one of their favourite

eating places, almost the first Christopher had taken her to, discreetly plush with a top-name chef. Although it was Friday night a table could be found for Mr Drayford and the soon-to-be Mrs Drayford, and when they walked in they were greeted with smiles from the staff and several of the diners.

In the Venetian mirror that dominated one wall Caroline saw their reflections as others were seeing them. They looked a well-dressed pair, and she thought, I am turning into an Anna Drayford clone. Another generation but out of the same mould.

She hadn't a hair out of place but in that fleeting glimpse it had seemed that her eyes were dark and restless. But she might have imagined that.

Nothing had changed since the last time they were here, a few weeks ago. They discussed the menu and sat back from their candle-lit table with their mouth-watering dishes and a good wine. They talked about themselves. Well, Christopher talked about where the honeymoon should be spent. This had been a lovely game for months now, because Caroline enjoyed hearing about the choices open to her, and tonight she listened and smiled and everywhere sounded wonderful. But not that important, as if she herself was not personally involved.

She was tired tonight, or the rich food and the wine and the lush ambience of the place were making her dopey, and she almost yawned once or twice, then pulled herself together because Christopher had been doing his best and he was beginning to slacken.

His worries were never far from his mind and at last he said glumly, 'Rafe's painting my mother.'

'What?' She had heard what he had said but the

name startled her as though it had been shouted in her
ear.

'Her portrait. That should keep him here for a
while.'

'It shouldn't take long. By the way, I mentioned a
clause of inheritance and he said if there was one he
wouldn't be looking for it, so he isn't staying.'

'He hadn't seen Isabel, then,' Christopher said.

'He didn't seem to know Isabel had phoned.' Life
was surging into her. She was waking with a vengeance.

'He does now,' said Christopher. 'He was out riding
this morning and my mother wasn't too sure about it.
Married woman and all that. But she's thought it over
since, she's asked Isabel over and Rafe doesn't seem to
mind. Isabel could keep him here.'

Caroline had been eating chicken with a lemon and
cream sauce. The flavour was delicate but suddenly her
palate was flooded with flavour as if her taste buds had
been activated. And her hearing and sight seemed
sharper. She had snapped out of lassitude into being
suddenly and fiercely alive with a new and frightening
emotion.

She was *jealous*! It was a small word for something
that could shake you from head to foot, and that was
so unexpected when you had never encountered it
before. Never with Christopher. She loved
Christopher, but if she had seen him making passionate
love to another woman it would not have shattered her
like the idea of Rafe meeting Isabel again.

The shock had been explosive. She felt as if she was
scurrying around trying to pick up the little pieces of
her life. They were sharp and splintered and smashed
beyond repair.

Incredibly, nothing had smashed around her. In the

candle-light the colour that flamed and ebbed in her face went unnoticed. Her clenched fingers slowly relaxed. Her voice was low and she seemed to be listening and smiling still, finishing her main course and choosing an ice for dessert, sipping coffee.

She was desperate to be alone, but she saw the meal out and sat in the car as they drove home, making the occasional comment that kept Christopher talking. Until he turned into the drive of Virginia Grove instead of going straight up the high street to Caroline's home.

Then she sat up in her seat. 'I wanted to go home.' She sounded like a tired child, and he said,

'My mother wants to see you about guests for our engagement party.'

'Tonight?'

'It's not that late.'

She could have sworn it was after midnight but it was not yet ten o'clock, and a house party three weeks ahead would be an urgent matter for Anna Drayford.

'I could write my list out for her,' muttered Caroline. There might not be an engagement party. She had to be alone to decide what she was going to do.

'Just half an hour,' Christopher said. She could have opened the door and run but she stayed where she was, shaking with inner crazy laughter. . .'I'm keeping away from you,' she had shouted, and Rafe had called back, 'You're welcome to try.'

She *was* trying, but even Christopher was against her, delivering her to the house where Anna was waiting, and Rafe would be there. Isabel might have dashed right over; she didn't live that far away. Caroline remembered Elpida with Rafe's arm around her. Tonight it would be Isabel, and Caroline felt utterly alone.

The family was there. Anna, Robert and Rafe. Nobody else. And at the far end of the long drawing-room they made a charming group—the beautiful setting, the distinguished-looking woman and the older man. And the younger man, handsome as the devil lounging in a dark red leather armchair.

They all turned as Christopher and Caroline entered the room, hand in hand. They all smiled, but Rafe's smile was different; cold, almost cruel, sending a chill through Caroline. She thought, He knew I would have to come although I don't want to be here, but he mustn't know how he could have me trapped.

He got up as soon as they reached the group but it seemed to Caroline that he stood up and walked towards her as soon as she entered the room, and that he had gripped her wrist hard, numbing the light contact of Christopher's fingers. In fact he had not touched her at all, but his power over her was petrifying.

Anna had moved along a little on the faded rose brocaded sofa, patting a cushion for Caroline to sit down beside her, and as soon as Caroline did she began talking about the party. Their usual caterers were always reliable. She had phoned some of her friends already but they must get the invitations out. In the run-up to Christmas most of their friends would have full diaries, but even a small get-together would be pleasant.

Anna did not mention that the real attraction would be Rafe. They would be flocking to see him again, cancelling other appointments. But of course it was Christopher's and Caroline's engagement party too, and Caroline would be the perfect young hostess as always. 'Now, who do you want to invite?' Anna asked her.

Caroline had always had friends, but not on the Drayford scale where acquaintances counted as friends. 'Come in tomorrow,' said Anna graciously, 'and we'll send out the invitations.' It was Saturday tomorrow, the shop closed early, but Caroline honestly did not know if she could go through with this.

On a low table in front of Rafe's chair was a pad on which he had been making head and shoulder sketches. She glanced down at it then up at Anna, getting the talk off engagement parties. 'Christopher tells me you're having your portrait done.' She almost looked at Rafe. 'You do portraits?'

'I've moved on from caricatures,' he said. 'Another case of making amends.' Then he picked up the sketch-pad and leaned across to offer it to her, and Anna asked,

'What do you think?'

Anna was obviously delighted and with good reason. The sketches were brilliant. They brought out the good bone-structure of her face. Anna Drayford as she must always have wanted to be, making her beautiful without obvious flattery. When the painting was finished it would give more pleasure than the full-length horse-faced portrait of her as a débutante.

This *is* amends for the caricatures, thought Caroline, turning pages, although they didn't know the caricatures existed. 'Shall I paint you?' said Rafe, and she almost dropped the pad.

'No, thank you.'

'But that's a wonderful idea.' Anna was almost clapping her hands, applauding it. 'We could be painted together.' She could be hoping to keep Rafe here longer, or maybe she did fancy a mother and 'daughter' study. There were several of them around the house: Victorian, Georgian, one in Jacobean ruffled collars in front of the wall-safe in the dining-room from which Rafe had taken the money after that row with his father. Caroline wondered if he was paying that back; it had been a tidy sum.

'No, thank you,' she said again, 'I'm not even photogenic. I'd hate to have my portrait painted.'

She did, in fact, take a good photograph, but she could never sit still while Rafe watched her for hours. He had the pad back now, sketching her, and she howled, '*No*!' glaring to emphasise her protest.

'That's good,' he nodded approvingly, 'a character study,' and she immediately went mask-like.

It was a lightning sketch, that quick, but as she sat frozen it seemed to Caroline that she was a prisoner here as she had been in the gazebo. But when he came across to her, his fingers holding her chin, turning her face, loosening strands of hair, she had to dig her nails into the palms of her hands or she might have covered his fingers with her own, holding his touch.

When he put down the sketchpad his mother picked it up and, after a moment, she said, 'That's—beautiful,' but she seemed slightly puzzled. Christopher and his father were looking at it and it was in front of Caroline.

Just a sketch, instantly recognisable, but of a transformed Caroline, with shining eyes, loose hair, bare shoulders—as it was head and shoulders it could have been a nude—and a butterfly just above her left breast: Caroline gone wild.

Christopher said, 'A butterfly?'

'Symbolic,' said Rafe and Caroline tried to laugh.

'That I have a butterfly mind?'

She had a small rosy birthmark just there. Rafe had seen it when he was smoothing in the oil and tonight she didn't much care who knew about that, although tomorrow she might resent being provoked like this.

'We could have you holding a lily,' he suggested, 'or a hunting knife?'

She was getting used to Christopher wondering what they were talking about, and when Rafe drew in a single line of a mountain background behind her—like the Danni and Giorgio sketches—Christopher asked, 'Is that supposed to be Crete?'

'Of course,' said Rafe.

He was making mischief and she should be saying something tactful, but right now the danger of him was like knocking back champagne, making her reckless so that she nearly burst out laughing. Although when Christopher said, 'I'll take you home,' she said,

'Yes, please; goodnight everyone.'

Rafe said nothing. His narrowed eyes glittered and he turned away as Anna said, 'You will be here tomorrow afternoon and if you could have your list ready. . .'

'I will,' Caroline murmured. She had had all she could take tonight but tomorrow she must decide if she was the daughter Anna wanted, the wife Christopher deserved.

His car was standing outside in the forecourt and they drove the few minutes to Caroline's home in silence. Tonight Christopher turned off the road into the yard behind the shop, switching off the engine and saying abruptly, 'I don't want him painting you.' Neither did she—there would be no argument there. 'I don't like the way he looks at you,' said Christopher. 'The way he touches you. He carries on as if he's taking you over.' His voice rose like someone losing a possession. 'It's not fair,' and she said wryly,

'As well as Virginia Grove?'

'As if he's got the whip hand everywhere. There is something going on between you, isn't there?'

'Maybe.' What else could she say?

Christopher groaned, 'He's told you.'

'Told me what?'

'About the money.'

She had to be punch-drunk. She could only think that Robert Drayford had made something over to Rafe: property, stocks, shares. Then Christopher said, 'I took it,' and her mind cleared so that she knew what he was going to say before he said it. 'When he took off I opened the safe and took the case. I needed it; I'd got debts and there were some tough characters after me. And if you'd heard the row you'd have thought he'd never be coming back.'

'So it didn't matter if they thought he was a thief?' She couldn't keep the scorn out of her voice, but Christopher almost laughed.

'Not that much. He was angry enough to have taken it—he was mad enough to have burned the house down. And look how things are now. It doesn't matter because it was Rafe, and Rafe can get away with murder. If they knew I'd once lost a small fortune on the horses and then emptied the wall-safe I'd be finished. All I've got going for me is I'm reliable. They'd never trust me again.'

She said, 'That's not true,' as if he was very young and she was comforting him, and he asked, like the very young,

'You won't tell them, will you?'

'Of course not.'

He still sounded hopeless. 'I don't think Rafe will either, but he's making me pay. That's why he's showing me he could get you to dump me. Not because he wants you. I don't think he wants Virginia Grove either. It all adds up to him calling in a debt I owe him.'

# CHAPTER EIGHT

'IT COULD be,' Caroline said quietly. She was cold and calm, in deep shock because this could explain so much. No wonder Christopher was paranoid about keeping Rafe away. If Anna and Robert Drayford knew that Christopher had been cheating them all these years they would be bitterly angry—they might even decide he should not inherit—so the money lifted from the wall-safe explained Christopher's attitude

And Rafe's? Rafe knew, of course. It had to have been mentioned when Anna's earlier reproachful letters reached him and he must have guessed who had taken it. He was cynical, unshockable, but he must have resented the assumption that he had to be the thief.

He didn't want Virginia Grove and all that went with it, but there was black humour as well as revenge in showing Christopher how easily Rafe could have taken over everything Christopher owned or hoped to own.

Including Caroline. 'He's showing me he could get you to dump me,' Christopher had just said. 'Not because he wants you. . .'

There had been no tenderness. It had been nearer anger. She remembered the smile that was no smile as Rafe had waited for her to reach him tonight, with Christopher holding her hand. She was twisting the ring on her finger, and Christopher was muttering miserably, 'You despise me, don't you?'

'No!' She could only feel shock, but she knew that

some time she would be sorry and sad for Christopher. He had paid for that opportunist theft. He must have woken sweating from nightmares of his brother coming back, knowing that if Rafe accused him the truth would out.

Now he put his hand over hers as she turned the ring. 'Please don't,' he whispered.

'What?'

'You want to take off the ring, don't you? You want to walk away.'

'Yes.' That was what she wanted. To give Christopher his ring, get out of this car, and never see another Drayford as long as she lived.

But he was pleading, 'Let's get the engagement party over,' and she stared because that seemed the least of their problems. 'My mother's been phoning all her friends. If I go back now and tell them the engagement's off it might suit Rafe but my parents would be shattered. I know Rafe is pressuring you, but please wait until he's gone and see how you feel then.'

Rafe would roar with laughter at the hypocrisy that made Christopher reluctant to cancel the engagement party. But the publicity and embarrassment that would cause would infuriate Anna, and Christopher would get the brunt of her rage as well as the humiliation of his brother being around to see Caroline dumping him. She couldn't hurt Christopher like that and she said, 'All right, then, we'll wait. Then if you like you can decide I'm not right for you. I'm not, you know, and there are lots of girls who are.'

'Thank you.' He was mightily relieved to leave things as they were for now and hope for the best for the future. As she stepped out of the car he kissed her an undemanding goodnight and said, 'You will come up tomorrow afternoon?'

'To go over the guest list with your mother? I'll be there, and don't worry—I won't let you down.'

'This is just a bad patch,' he said. 'Nothing has happened.'

She nodded and let herself into the house. There was no one down here; her parents were in bed although they had left the light on in the little sitting-room. She heard the car start up and drive away, and then she switched off the downstairs light and went upstairs.

Just a bad patch, Christopher had said. Patches were small, but this one was big enough to turn into a black hole in space and swallow her whole. Nothing has happened, Christopher had said, and that was a laugh when she felt as if every cell in her body had changed until nothing remained of the girl she had been.

She almost laughed, with fingers pressed against her mouth. But she stopped that before the sob in her throat got out, and went slowly and doggedly through getting ready for bed.

It was a long time before she slept, and although she had plenty to think about none of her thinking served any purpose because there was nothing she could do to change a thing. . .

Saturday morning started like every other morning, with Caroline gulping her coffee and carrying a piece of toast around with her while she put a couple of fashion magazines into her briefcase and answered a phone call from a girlfriend.

Her father was halfway through the cooked breakfast his wife had prepared for him almost every morning of their married life when Caroline was on her way out of the house, telling her mother, 'I'm going straight to the Grove from work; I don't know when I'll be home.'

Mary Hammond smiled because this was what she liked to hear, reminding her that her daughter was at home in Virginia Grove and almost Mrs Christopher Drayford.

Caroline had no idea how she was going to explain to them, I don't love Christopher. Well, I do love him the way I have always loved him, but it isn't nearly enough, and if he and his mother and father came to know me well they would be clawing this ring back.

'What about the wedding-dress?' Sally asked later as she followed Caroline into the little office where it was still hanging.

'Very lily-like', Rafe had said. 'I don't think so,' said Caroline, and Sally closed the door, her eyes bright with curiosity.

'And what about Rafe Drayford? What about him coming here for you yesterday?'

'What about it?' said Caroline

'Well, I mean, you met him in Crete, didn't you? And something brought him home again for the first time in years. Well. . .' She waited.

Sally had always been a good friend. Some time Caroline would tell her that her engagement to Christopher was in trouble, but she couldn't talk about Rafe. She shrugged and said, 'He's here, but he'll soon be gone. And he won't leave a forwarding address.'

'Shame,' Sally sighed, then grinned. 'He wouldn't be asking you to go with him?' and before Caroline could say, Don't be daft, Sally said, 'That's a silly idea, isn't it? You've got it made here and you're not the roving kind.'

Caroline had worked in this shop since she had left

school, but before long she might start looking for
work and accommodation in another town. That might
be her only escape from the gossip and well-meaning
advice that would overwhelm her as soon as she broke
away from the Drayfords of Virginia Grove.

This morning she scribbled her guest list for Anna
Drayford, reflecting wryly that, as there was going to
be no wedding, her friends might as well enjoy the
party on offer. She busied herself with business matters
and when the shop closed at midday she stayed on until
the lunch-hour was over.

She had to spend an hour or two with Anna this
afternoon but she was avoiding what might be a family
meal. She was determined to dodge Rafe, and she
would have preferred to keep clear of Christopher. But
Christopher was waiting for her.

As her car drew up in front of the house he came
hurrying out to kiss her. 'Thank you, darling,' he said.
For wearing the ring while Rafe was here, he meant,
and maybe forever; and she almost said, You're asking
too much; I'm through with the lot of you.

But she was in the house by now. 'She's in the small
parlour,' Christopher was telling her, and that was
where Caroline had expected Anna Drayford to be
because the small parlour was her office-cum-sitting-
room.

It was a charming room, overlooking a courtyard of
garages and stable block. Anna dealt with correspon-
dence at the rosewood bureau and held committee
meetings in here for her various charities, or served tea
to a few friends because the chintz-covered chairs were
deep and comfortable.

She was at the bureau now, papers in front of her,

and Rafe was standing by the window. 'Got the list?' he asked Caroline.

'Yes.'

He was in riding gear—breeches, boots, hacking jacket. A rich man's version of a mountain man's outfit. Nobody else seemed to be in the room. Just Rafe and herself, and they could have been on a mountain-top so far as Caroline was concerned because the only thing she could see clearly was the tall dark man. When Anna Drayford asked, 'How about the wedding, Rafe? You'll come to the wedding?' her voice seemed very far away.

'You have a date fixed?' Rafe was still looking at Caroline, but it was Anna who answered,

'Caroline is going to be a spring bride.'

'Charming! Can I give the bride away?'

'You have as much chance of that as you have of being the best man,' Caroline said, and when he laughed she did too, although she was near to screaming.

Anna was smiling and saying, 'We don't need you men here, either of you. This is serious business; just leave us to it.'

Christopher put a hand on Caroline's shoulder now but she hardly felt his touch. 'See you later, then?' said Christopher.

'What? Oh, yes.'

Rafe had been riding or was going riding, and again she could feel his long hard body against hers as if he held her in his arms. 'Coming?' he said.

He should have been speaking to Christopher but he was still looking at Caroline. 'Riding,' he said, 'over the hills.' He had to be joking, and somehow she kept her voice light.

'Horses bounce me off. I'd rather walk.'

'I remember,' he said. He must be remembering how she had described the walks she took, alone over the moors, when he had told her about the fiesta in Peru and she had imagined being there with him.

She knew now why listening to Christopher talking about faraway places last night had seemed impersonal. It was because she was going nowhere with Christopher. Nor with Rafe, but wherever she went it would be hard to keep Rafe out of her mind.

She took the list out of her handbag and put it by the papers before Anna Drayford, and both men went out of the room while their mother was glancing down the names, nodding at some, looking blank at others, the ones Anna Drayford had never heard of till now. But it was a short list and of course Caroline's friends were welcome here.

She was given a stack of Anna's invitation cards to fill in with dates and details and she sat at a little table by the window, writing cards for Sally and the girls in the shop, although she would be seeing them all on Monday and could easily have asked them then.

Rafe was in the courtyard below, astride the big black stallion, talking with the groom. As he rode away he looked up and waved as if he had known Caroline was watching him. Although she hardly was; she had just glanced down. She didn't wave back, but ducked her head, and he had gone anyway.

Anna Drayford was finding Caroline useful as a private secretary, training her to help in all sorts of little chores. Now Anna went through the names on the main guest list, giving Caroline run-downs on the guests she had not yet met, coming at last and inevitably to the girl who had been Isabel Faulkner.

'You remember Isabel?' said Anna.

'I've never actually met her.'

'A lovely girl.' Anna's smile was wistful. 'Such silly misunderstandings. Rafe should have married her,' she said, and the headache that had nagged Caroline faintly all morning took a sudden leap and began to throb.

'She did get married, you know,' Anna said confidentially. 'Two years ago. But it wasn't a success, so perhaps. . .who knows? She's coming tomorrow. You will be here, won't you, tomorrow afternoon? You could end up as sisters; wouldn't that be lovely?'

That would be bloody marvellous, Caroline almost said. God, she thought, you are such a stupid cow. I don't care what you think—he is not going to settle down with Isabel.

What he might do, of course, was join Isabel in a brief and blazing affair before he took off again. That would be in character and it could be what Isabel expected, and good luck to them both.

Except that luck was the last thing Caroline was wishing. Her stomach was churning and an ache was pounding in her skull—she felt as if she had taken poison, but she stayed a little longer. She could hardly run out of the room, although as soon as she possibly could she stood up and said, 'This is in hand now, isn't it? I do have another appointment.'

Anna was so taken aback that she was still murmuring huffily, 'Do you? Oh, I'm sorry, you should have said it was inconvenient,' as Caroline closed the door behind her.

Christopher followed her out of the house and she told him, 'I have to go. I've got to get back into town. Business.'

'May I come?'

'No.' He was anxious to cause no trouble and she gave him no time to say any more before she drove off and left him standing. She parked her car well out of the village and off the road, on rough grass near one of the paths that led up into the hills.

Once stag and wild boar had been hunted here, when it was all part of the Drayford estates. Some land and properties still belonged to them, leased mostly to local farmers. Some was covered with dark fir plantations. But there were still miles of more or less open heathland, and the occasional isolated cottage, Drayford owned, let out to holiday tenants.

Caroline set off at a brisk pace. She had a few hours left before nightfall and although the chances of finding a lone rider out here were slim she might as well start looking, because she had to get to him some time.

She could not bear the thought of him with Isabel. Or with any woman. Not making love. Not in real, if transient, intimacy. The thought of that hurt with a physical pain that made her stop sometimes and hunch over tightly folded arms as if the poison was killing her.

All the while her eyes searched for a moving figure. She stayed on the route she had described to him. He'd keep out of the gorse and waist-high heather, and he might not be taking a horse over the more uneven ground which was frozen rock-hard. But she was wearing stupid shoes for hiking, although it was too late to worry about that, and when she reached a small rock formation that gave her a slight vantage point she climbed to the flat top of the tallest and squinted at the horizon.

Almost at once she saw the rider on the dark horse, and he saw her right away and came galloping towards her. She had told Rafe about the rock in the Cornish bay, to which she had swum in the moonlight. 'Wel-

come to my rock,' she had said. She might say that
now. It could be a way to recapture a happy moment if
she could smile and joke.

But when he reined in the horse, his eyes almost
level with hers as she stood on her rock top, she
couldn't smile, and she could only say what she had
come out here to ask. 'Don't you think it's about time
you told me what is really going on?'

He reached across to haul her up beside him as she
protested, 'I told you, I'm not too brilliant on a horse.'

'That's all right,' he said, 'I am. Get astride.'

'I—can't.' Her skirt, under her top coat was tight.

'Of course you can.' His supporting hand gripped
her shoulder while she wriggled, nearly dropping her
bag and losing her shoes, but finally finishing, with her
skirt well above her knees, more or less astride the
broad back of the horse. 'Just hang on,' he said, and
that advice she didn't need.

She had never been on a horse this high; the hard
frozen ground seemed a long way down, and she clung
on to him for dear life, her teeth chattering. 'Why—
couldn't we have talked here?'

'It looks like snow.'

'Does it?' It was cold enough and the skies were
heavy. 'Well, why couldn't I have walked?'

'This is quicker.'

She had never really mastered the rhythm of riding
even on a slow and gentle mount, and now she was
bouncing about with not enough breath left to do more
than gasp, 'What *is* going on?' although she probably
wouldn't hear half he said, the way her face was
bumping against his back.

'This time I am abducting you,' he said. 'An old
Cretan custom but we'll give it a fling.'

She was in no mood for joking. As soon as she was on firm ground the questions she had to ask could bring answers that would leave her feeling she would never smile again. But for now she had to hang on to him and hang on to her bag, gritting her teeth and praying they weren't going far. She couldn't even get out the question, *Where?*

It was far enough, two or three miles and off the beaten track. Once this had been a smallholding. All but the flagstoned yard had gone back to heather but the white-walled cottage seemed in good repair, and when Rafe reined in the horse, dismounted and reached up to help her down, she stared around blearily.

She had never come this close to the buildings. She knew it was a holiday let, usually for riding holidays, horses or ponies being hired from a nearby riding school, but it looked empty. Curtains were drawn and no smoke rose from the chimney, although it was a bitterly cold day, and yet she was shaken, hot and bothered from getting here.

Rafe was handing her a key. 'You go inside,' he said. 'I'll see to Brummel.'

An outbuilding was a stable and she turned a key in the green-painted door of the house. It turned easily, the lock being well oiled, and the room into which she stepped smelt of lavender, polish or potpourri.

She opened the curtains and saw a fair-sized farm-house-type kitchen, with a solid fuel range, old pine table, chairs and dresser, bright rugs on the red-tiled floor. Arriving here on holiday, you would be pleased, feeling welcomed, hurrying to try out the oil-lamps and light the fire to bring the house to life.

Crazily she thought, If I had married Christopher I

might have asked for this for my own, as a wedding present. It would make a smashing hideout.

Her head was still spinning from bouncing around on Brummel and she wondered if she was bruised. She wondered what she was doing here, why she had set off over the moors searching for Rafe, because when she talked to him it would have been better to look composed and less like that sketch with the mountain ridge as background.

She was muffled up today, no bare shoulders, no butterfly for a birthmark, but her hair had been blown wild and lord knew what he would read in her eyes. There had to be a bathroom with a mirror—she had a mirror in her bag—but she couldn't face herself even to smooth down her hair.

She looked at the room instead, examining willow-patterned cups and saucers and plates on the dresser, Victorian prints on the walls: two girls in sun-bonnets wandering down a country lane, an old woman at a spinning wheel in a kitchen rather like this, horses hunting, racing. The cold began to get to her again and she knew she was scared, wondering what he would say.

So that when he came into the house she was shivering, and he went to the range, opening an iron door and putting a match to a fire that was already laid. She asked, 'Do you come here often?' and her voice would have shaken if she hadn't been careful.

'I looked the place up again,' he said. 'It's kept habitable all year round. Folk come here for Christmas holidays. Families from town fancy Christmas in the country, with fir trees on their doorstep.'

She had known that, but this was the first time she had been in one of the Drayford cottages on the moors.

As the flames flickered she would have liked to hold out her hands to them, but that would have meant kneeling down beside him and that could be playing with a fiercer fire.

She was so nervous that she couldn't stop shaking or chattering, and she babbled, 'You didn't even have to chop up a chair to get this fire started.'

'Sit down,' he said and she sat down in one of the chairs by the table. 'Now,' he said, 'what do you want to know?'

She wanted to know if Christopher was right about what had brought Rafe home. If Rafe wanted to see Isabel again. How he felt about Isabel. How he felt about Caroline. She swallowed and said, 'Christopher told me about the money in the wall-safe.'

'What about it?'

'That he took it.'

'That was rash of him.' Rafe sounded amused. 'On both counts. Taking it and telling you. Why *did* he tell you?'

'He thought you might have done. And he's worried what your parents would think if they knew.'

'I'll bet he is.' Rafe got up from the fireplace and his grin would have alarmed Christopher, but then he went on, 'Only I won't be telling them. They've had no difficulty casting me as the guilty party all these years, and I don't give a damn, so why reopen the case?'

'Don't you *care*?' Forgiveness like this would have been saintly, and he was no saint.

'Of course I did. I was bloody angry.' She wished he would sit down instead of standing because he was so tall that it cricked her neck to look up at him. 'That's why I never came back and hardly kept in touch. I hadn't taken their money, although I'd earned some of it. And if I'd taken anything it wouldn't have been like a thief in the night.'

The way Christopher must have taken it, silently, secretly, scared out of his wits and his conscience by the men who were threatening him if he didn't pay up, scared ever since that Rafe would deny it and he would be accused.

Then Rafe laughed and came and sat beside her. 'It has its funny side. My father must have thought it proved his point. He told me I'd end up in jail during the last row.'

'The big one?' This was easier than she had expected. She could almost have put a hand on his arm. She did lean towards him, smiling.

'They couldn't have come much bigger,' he agreed cheerfully. 'Not without blood on the carpet.'

'Christopher said you were mad enough to burn the house down.'

'Christopher was always given to eavesdropping,' he said, and then, 'No, that's not fair. Everyone in the house must have heard—we were roaring at each other like wounded bulls. I wonder my father didn't have a seizure, poor old devil, although at the time I could happily have murdered him.'

'What did it in the end? What sparked it off?'

They were in league again, together, friends if nothing more, and when he said, 'The lovely Isabel,' she could have yelped with joy. 'They had me married. Isabel. My folk, her folk. I was in for chairman of the board, the keys to the castle. Everything settled, while I'd been walking around like a zombie.'

She laughed then, throwing back her head and pealing with laughter. 'And that's when he told you you'd end in jail?'

'That's when I told him I'd rather go to jail. "That's where you'll end," he said. "That's where I've been in this house," I said. ' He laughed with her. 'The rest is history.'

She said gaily, 'But it isn't over. She's coming tomorrow.'

'So they tell me.'

'And she's still a lovely girl. I've got your mother's word for that. Your mother, who still thinks it was all a silly misunderstanding and you should have married her.'

He still smiled, but suddenly his eyes were watchful and his voice was quiet. 'Did you come out here to ask me if I was going to blow Chris's little secret?'

'What?' She had forgotten the money and Christopher, but she remembered why she had come. 'I came to ask you if you were considering an affair with Isabel?'

As she looked into his eyes her senses were beginning to swim, as if she was being drawn again somewhere beyond conscious thought. His mouth was strong and sensual and beautiful. She watched his mouth as he said, 'If I have an affair with anyone it will be with you,' and her own lips shaped the words,

'That has been on the cards.'

'For a long time,' he said. 'But I can't take much more of this, so far and no further.'

They were leaning towards each other, so close that they breathed each other's breath. 'I think I want you,' she said.

'I think that you do.' His skin and his breath were cold and clean but when she did touch him she might go up in flames. 'Because we could have set the mountains on fire,' he said. 'But there is a condition.'

He spoke slowly, deliberately. 'You think you want me——' she gave a small nod '—but I know that the way I feel about you goes deeper and needs more. Ours wouldn't be an affair but a commitment. Because if I make love to you I'll never let you go again.'

She was so dazed that she might have been dreaming. 'Do you want to discuss this?' he said.

Discuss it? Of course she did; the talking would be wonderful, but now she was speaking another language. Her hands were behind his head and magnetism, electricity, whatever, was fusing them together. They stood up and a chair crashed back, and he was crushing her as if they clung together in a hurricane.

The wind blew them, she was sure it did, through a door, and then she was lying on a bed and her covering was blowing away as she undid and unwrapped, or he did, throwing clothing aside. She watched spellbound as he stripped, her hair falling over her eyes like a veil, because he was everything she wanted, in every way a magnificent man. She had always known he was but she would never tire of looking at him.

Then he came to her, and his hand stroking her face brought a surge of pure joy, so that she closed her eyes with a gasp and then a little moan of delight. And there was a discussion of sorts, what hands meant, what lips meant, as his mouth caressed her shoulders, feathering the birthmark, kissing away the ache in her breasts.

And everywhere he touched the aching became a little trail of fire until she was in a white heat for him, pulling him towards her, moving with him, her nails clawing his shoulders, her fingertips digging into the hard muscles of back and buttocks.

She had never known nor dreamt that her body was capable of such fierce pleasure. She was superwoman, she was the brightest new star in the galaxy, reaching what seemed to be the limits of bearable rapture and then soaring higher, to another peak, another summit of ecstasy.

Beyond sensual hunger this was a wild and wonderful togetherness, and the climax that came at last was like arriving at paradise. . .such joy, such fulfilment, such love.

She shuddered into melting stillness in his arms, and lay for a while because her eyelids were too heavy to lift. When she looked into his face her heartbeats quickened so that her naked breasts must show the rise and fall, and she put up a hand as some sort of cover.

'That always was an ugly ring,' he said.

Harriet's ring. Christopher's ring. She said, 'I tried to give it back to him yesterday but he asked me to go on wearing it until after the engagement party.'

'I'm very glad you were giving it back.' He smiled the crooked smile and for her his eyes smiled too. 'But why does he want an engagement party?'

'He's scared your mother would go spare with the social embarrassment of calling it off at this stage. We were going to stop being engaged in a few months' time.'

'You are joking.'

'No, I'm not.'

'As I said before, not much changes here. You wouldn't have enjoyed living in the Grove.'

She might have done if she had not met him in the White Mountains, although this passion in her must have been inborn, well under the surface but strong and waiting. And some time Rafe would have come, or somewhere they would have met and recognised each other and known they had to be together.

'It's snowing,' he said.

Beyond the windowpanes white flakes were swirling, and the room was cold. She hadn't noticed that until now. Nor that the bed had only a counterpane on the mattress—no blankets or sheets. He picked up clothes for her and she got into enough to keep out the chill; undies, sweater and skirt.

Then they sat feet up, on the bed again, and watched the snow coming down, his arm around her, her head against his shoulder. 'If it goes on like this,' she said, 'it will be like the hamlet.'

Of course, this isolation was nothing compared to the immense loneliness of the mountains, but they had had a little house up there and it had been the beginning. She said, 'Maybe we should have stayed another day or so.'

'You wanted to come down.'

'Didn't you?'

'Well. . .yes.' She lifted her head to look at him, to tease,

'You don't sound too sure,' and he smoothed her hair off her forehead, away from her temples, tenderly, lovingly, telling her,

'When I turned back from checking if we could get down and saw you on the edge I was terrified. You weren't going to fall but for the moment I thought you were, and it was as if you were my woman, my love, about to go head first down a precipice. But you weren't mine, you were my brother's. That was when I decided we had to get down and I had to send you away. Because I wanted to keep you up there and do everything I could to make you forget Christopher.'

'Why didn't you?' His smile was a warmth over all of her, going deep, filling her with happiness.

'It didn't seem in your best interests,' he said. 'Also it seemed that I might be going mad.'

'A little.' But no madness was ever more sane. They smiled at each other, lazily, like lovers sharing every reason to smile.

He said, 'We got down, didn't we, and I kept my hands off you except in a purely professional way? Even when I brought up your supper tray.'

'It was a very good supper tray.'

'On the heavy side because I'd stacked it for two. Then when you looked at me I knew that if I stayed longer than a couple of minutes I'd try to make love to you and you would probably tell me to get the hell out of there, and I wanted you to leave liking me at least.'

He should have stayed. They should have shared that meal and that night, but it didn't matter now, and she was loving hearing him saying these things.

'I'm a rational man usually.' She nodded gravely. 'You'd had your excursion into the mountains, and you couldn't wait to get back to the easy life.'

She thought about that. 'I believe I did say that. Something to do with a hot bath. But you didn't ask me to stay.'

'There seemed no point.' His fingers were stroking her shoulders, drifting down her back. 'So you went, and by the end of that day I knew that I had to follow you. I didn't know where you'd gone, and you had left the island. But I knew you had to come home some time, so I came back and waited for you.'

No revenge. Even the London exhibition had not been the real priority. Sally, the romantic, was right: Rafe had come back for Caroline.

He said, 'I hoped you might not be sorry to see me, but when you came down that room with my mother

and Christopher you looked——' His grin was wry
with remembered pain. 'Well, there was no welcome
there.'

'I was scared.' She had been so confused. She spoke
fast, beginning to understand. 'When I was nearly
home, driving from the airport, I started to feel terribly
depressed. I couldn't think why but it was because I
didn't want what I thought was waiting for me—life at
the Grange. This.' She looked at the ring. 'Then when
I got here and you'd arrived I didn't know what was
happening.'

'I knew.' He looked grim now, in deadly earnest.
'You were wrong for Christopher but in every way you
and I belonged together. Every time he held your hand
I wanted to knock him away from you and grab and
shout, Look at me, listen to me, I'm the one you want.'

Heaven knew she was in earnest too, but the idea of
him doing that, in front of them all, made her lips
twitch. 'That would have stirred things up.'

'Would it have worked?'

'Very probably.' Shock treatment, but it might have
cleared her mind. 'But the slow stir was working. I was
handing the ring back.'

'Even this afternoon, seeing that on your hand hurt
like hell. And that engagement party list you
brought. . . I couldn't have gone through an engagement party; I'd have abducted you before then.'

She giggled, 'Like this?'

'Somewhere we could be alone. This does well
enough.'

'This does very well.'

'On a count of ten, nine and a half? God, was I
jealous!' They were both remembering and she knew
how jealousy hurt. Now she saw the lines round his

eyes as though he had not been getting much sleep lately, and when she reached up to smooth them away he caught her fingers and held them. 'I couldn't ask how lovemaking was with Christopher,' he said. 'I had to say sex because I couldn't use the word love. I only wanted you to love me. There is a difference. You do love me?'

His dark eyes were drawing her to him as they always would, and she said softly, 'Yes, I love you, and there is a difference.'

Even a kiss, deep and sweet, was enough to make the difference plain. Taking her in strong loving arms, whispering tender words, this man was giving her a rare happiness. Being held by him, she was wrapped in comfort like a lovely sleep, and perhaps she did sleep, because night was falling outside but the window was now encrusted with snow.

She yawned and said, 'You manage things so well; did you arrange the snow?'

He stretched luxuriously beside her. 'I could say yes, but you might ask me to stop it falling.'

Nobody would find them tonight or look for them. 'Let it fall,' she said, 'I quite like it.'

'Are you hungry?'

'What do we do, hunt a buzzard?'

He sighed in mock reproach. 'For a woman who was just suggesting I can fix the weather you lose faith fast. Of course we have food.' She gave a cheer. 'Don't get excited, it's store-cupboard stuff. Wait while I light a lamp.'

He went into the kitchen and when she followed him there was an oil-lamp burning. He was taking stocks from a cupboard and stacking them on the table, including a tin of sardines and a bottle of wine.

She picked up the sardines and read '"In olive oil". I don't have the stiffness this time and any bruises are from bouncing around on Brummel. Well, most of them.' Rafe was shirtless and she saw the scratches on his back. Had she done that? Her nails were not claw-like but she seemed to have left her mark. She winced and said, 'Sorry.'

'For what?'

'Scratches.' She brushed his shoulder blade with soft lips and he grinned.

'I did say you were a tiger. We open the sardines?'

'Of course.' They opened enough tins and packets to fill half a dozen plates, and the bottle of wine. Last night Caroline had eaten exquisitely cooked food with Christopher and most of it had seemed tasteless. Now everything was delicious. She savoured a morsel of sardine and said, 'St Teresa once said that it must have been something in her nature, but if anyone gave her so much as a sardine they could ask anything of her.'

'She must have been fond of sardines. You come out with some odd facts.'

'I'm quite well read,' she said gaily. 'I'm rather bright in my way.'

'You are incandescent in every way. Why do you think we only need one lamp in here?'

The fire threw out a red glow and the lamp on the table gave a yellow light, but she felt that happiness must light up the room. Her eyes were shining, and he said huskily, 'You are so beautiful. We'll have a marvellous life. I'll take you wherever you want to go. I'll take you to the Cave of the Winds.'

'Can we go back to the village?'

'Danni's granddaughter would always be welcome

and they'll let me back in.' He had no doubts on that
and neither had she. 'Elpida knew I would follow you.'

She was sorry for Elpida, but the young man who
had watched her dancing and sighed had been tall and
handsome. And Christopher would find another girl
who would be much better for him than Caroline. She
said, 'Christopher knew there was something between
us but he thought it was revenge.'

'What was?'

'You wanting me to break off the engagement to pay
him back for taking that money.'

He raised an eyebrow. 'That's not very logical, and
he's a lawyer. Still, what sort of reasoning can we
expect from a man who called you lily-girl?'

She put on a demure expression. 'Oh, I can look like
a lily.'

'So you can,' he said. 'You'll make a magical bride,'
and as her lips parted, 'I warned you I'd never let you
go. I can't imagine life without you because there
would be no life without you. We are married. We'll
go through the legalities as soon as we can but that is a
logical, irrefutable fact.'

It was. They were husband and wife and it was
wonderful. She slipped the ruby ring from her finger
and put it into his hand, and without looking away
from her he tossed it aside. It fell silently on one of the
rugs, and if it bounced or rolled neither of them knew
because they only had eyes for each other, although
after a few moments she smiled and said, 'I hope you
can find that again or the family who come here for
Christmas are going to think that Santa Claus is very
generous this year.'

'So he is. Wait until you see the ring you're getting.'

'It doesn't matter.'

'Yes, it does. But you can choose.'

It didn't matter, but she would like to wear his ring. Then she had to smile again. 'And what about that engagement party?'

'Let them come,' he said. 'We'll give them something to celebrate.'

He reached for her hands, drawing her to him, and reached for her lips. Outside the snow continued to fall, soft and deep, while inside Caroline and Rafe began their own night-long loving feast of celebration and thanksgiving for the life they would share through all the fabulous years to come.

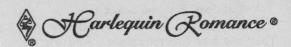

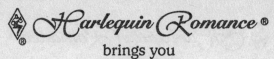

*Harlequin Romance* ®

brings you

## Some men are worth waiting for!

They're handsome, they're charming but, best of all, they're single! Twelve lucky women are about to discover that finding Mr. Right is not a problem—it's holding on to him.

In May the series continues with:

**#3408 MOVING IN WITH ADAM**
by Jeanne Allan

Hold out for Harlequin Romance's heroes in coming months...

♦ June: **THE DADDY TRAP**—Leigh Michaels

♦ July: **THE BACHELOR'S WEDDING**—Betty Neels

♦ August: **KIT AND THE COWBOY**—Rebecca Winters

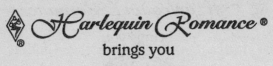

*Harlequin Romance* ®

brings you

## *How the West Was Wooed!*

We've rounded up twelve of our most popular authors, and the result is a whole year of romance, Western style. Every month we'll be bringing you a spirited, independent woman whose heart is about to be lassoed by a rugged, handsome, one-hundred-percent cowboy!

Watch for...

◆ May: **THE BADLANDS BRIDE**—Rebecca Winters

◆ June: **RUNAWAY WEDDING**—Ruth Jean Dale

◆ July: **A RANCH, A RING AND EVERYTHING**—Val Daniels

◆ August: **TEMPORARY TEXAN**—Heather Allison

Available wherever Harlequin books are sold.

# HARLEQUIN ✦ PRESENTS®

—where satisfaction is guaranteed!

Coming next month, two classic stories
by your favorite authors:

## *FORGOTTEN HUSBAND*
### by Helen Bianchin
Harlequin Presents #1809

They said he was her husband...

But Elise didn't feel married to Alejandro Santanas, or
the mother of his unborn child. The accident had destroyed
her memory of the past few months. Had she really been in
love with this handsome stranger—and would he expect
that passion again?

## *ONE NIGHT OF LOVE*
### by Sally Wentworth
Harlequin Presents #1810

Once bitten, twice shy!

Oliver Balfour was the most attractive man Dyan had ever
met. But she wasn't going to mix business with pleasure.
From experience Dyan knew that a man like Oliver
would stalk a woman like her by lying his way into her
affections...and then go quickly for the kill in her bed!

Harlequin Presents—the best has just gotten better!
Available in May wherever Harlequin books are sold.

## UNLOCK THE DOOR TO GREAT ROMANCE
## AT BRIDE'S BAY RESORT

Join Harlequin's new across-the-lines series, set
in an exclusive hotel on an island off the coast of
South Carolina.

Seven of your favorite authors will bring you exciting stories
about fascinating heroes and heroines discovering love at
Bride's Bay Resort.

Look for these fabulous stories coming to a store near you
beginning in January 1996.

**Harlequin American Romance #613 in January**
*Matchmaking Baby* by Cathy Gillen Thacker

**Harlequin Presents #1794 in February**
*Indiscretions* by Robyn Donald

**Harlequin Intrigue #362 in March**
*Love and Lies* by Dawn Stewardson

**Harlequin Romance #3404 in April**
*Make Believe Engagement* by Day Leclaire

**Harlequin Temptation #588 in May**
*Stranger in the Night* by Roseanne Williams

**Harlequin Superromance #695 in June**
*Married to a Stranger* by Connie Bennett

**Harlequin Historicals #324 in July**
*Dulcie's Gift* by Ruth Langan

Visit Bride's Bay Resort each month wherever
Harlequin books are sold.

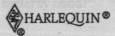